ROLLING ALL THE TIME

Stories by James Ballard

UNIVERSITY OF ILLINOIS PRESS

Urbana   Chicago   London

Manufactured in the United States of America

"Wild Honey" appeared first in the *Atlantic Monthly,* January 1966, © 1965 by The Atlantic Monthly Company. Reprinted with permission.

Epigraph from W. H. Auden, "Lullaby," *Collected Shorter Poems 1927-1957.* © 1967 Random House, Inc. Reprinted by permission of the publisher.

Library of Congress Cataloging in Publication Data

Ballard, James, 1921-
    Rolling all the time.

    (Illinois short fiction)
    CONTENTS: Introductory aeronautics.—Wild honey.—
The feast of Crispian.—Down by the riverside. [etc.]
    I. Title.
PZ3.B2121Ro [PS3503.A55717]   813'.5'4   76-13475
ISBN 0-252-00613-5
ISBN 0-252-00614-3 pbk.

In memoriam
GMB   CRB

And for Mayo Kimbrell

Noons of dryness see you fed
By the involuntary powers,
Nights of insult let you pass
Watched by every human love.
　　　　　—W. H. Auden

Contents

Introductory Aeronautics

From the way she was sitting on the culvert railing, Russ could see that something had happened to her. For her to be sitting there at all, on the bridge rail, meant something had gone wrong. He was on his way down Newton Avenue, a steep slope, with the culvert at the bottom of it. Hurrying now. Their house was only two blocks from where she was, and if she could not get that much farther, something serious was the matter.

He started running. His shoe sole, the left one, came loose again, and it was flopping. He was calling to her then, and then he had reached her. "Mom? You all right? What is it?"

In a minute, she put a hand towards him. It was the way somebody blind would put out a hand. She had taken hold of him then, and her face was against his dirty jacket.

It was embarrassing. They were out here where anybody could see them, and she was going on with all this.

But then he had put his arms around her. And it was both of them. Out here in public.

"Russell Kaiser. Why didn't you let somebody know. So we could be expecting you."

"What were you sitting on the railing for?"

"When you came around the corner up there. And it surprised me so. And I had to find something as quick as I could, to—. Russell Kaiser. Why didn't you let somebody know."

She had already seen him before he had known he was in sight.

"But it's all right, Russell. That's all right, you hear? You didn't need to let us know. Just so you're back, is what matters. I was going across the bridge here, Russell. I was just now on my way to work, and when I looked up, there you were. I thought maybe I was making it up. And when I realized I wasn't, I had to sit down, you see, as quick as I could."

He felt strange himself that he was here. And yet, as if he had known it for a long time. When he was getting near town earlier in the afternoon, the trip nearly over, nearly over, actually and in fact all but finished, he kept having the same feeling that used to happen when he would dream he had become able to fly. Become able again. Remembered how. But he would wake up, and have to realize again that he had only been dreaming, been suckered in again.

She was calm now. She smiled at him.

He felt himself smiling. But it went away, for he saw now how thin she was, and anxious. Much thinner than when he had left.

He had been to Florida, to a place his father's sister had down there. Her name was Metta. She had a nut farm, a pecan ranch, out from the town of Palatka. He had not given Metta the news he was leaving, when he left, and evidently she had not let his mother, or even his father, know he was gone.

"Let's get on to the house, Russell. Everybody's going to want to see you. Look at us, standing out here on the street."

There was a package on the sidewalk. A small one, wrapped in newspaper. He picked it up.

"Yes, thanks. That's just some—that's a little lunch I take along with me to work. Your shoe, Russell. The sole is almost off."

"Just about."

He had a lot of mileage on that shoe. On both of them. He had thumbed rides up here from Palatka, and now and then between rides, instead of waiting, he had walked. They had been an old pair already. Walking gave him the feeling of getting something done. Of getting home quicker. The trip had taken him four days and three nights, in all. Palatka, Florida, to Pittsburgh, Pennsylvania.

The house they were passing now was the Haynes house. Or it used to be. It was empty, and it had a For Rent placard on the front

door. He wondered when Mr. and Mrs. Haynes had moved. One
night last fall, one of the bad ones, Mr. Haynes had come to their
house and calmed his father down. His father was not going to want
to see him, especially. She had said everybody was.

"Is the old man around, Mom?"

She stopped. "Russell? Didn't you know?—Your father, Russell.
Not the old man. Didn't Metta tell you about him?"

"Tell me what?"

"Your father isn't here anymore, Russell. He left. I thought you
knew about it. I wrote to you about it. I wrote to Metta, and I wrote
to you . . . You never got the letter, did you?"

"I never got a letter about that, Mom."

"And she never told you."

"What happened to him?"

"He just left, Russell. Right after Christmas, not a word to anybody. We haven't heard from him. I thought maybe he'd gone to
visit Metta himself, or dropped her a line about it, but she said he
hadn't. I did get a letter from her about that. It's peculiar she didn't
say anything about it to you."

"She never did."

They were walking again. She was holding his arm. "Russell. Did
she treat you all right, while you were there?"

"It wasn't not all right. I had to do everything she said. She had
rules for everything. Like he did."

"Yes. Yes, they were both always like that."

Metta would say sometimes that the principal cause of all the
trouble was his mother. "I'm thoroughly aware of that. Why,
Brother was one of the sweetest people anybody would wish to
know." She referred to his father as Brother. One of his upper front
teeth was missing, from the time Brother knocked it out one night
last fall, the time Mr. Haynes came to the house, and when Metta
asked him about it was when she had mentioned again that his
mother was the cause of the trouble.

"Where you working, Mom? You said you were on the way to
work?"

"I'm at the Snow White, Russell. That's the Snow White Laundry,

over on Seeger Avenue. I'm almost ashamed to tell you. What I do,
I'm a picker."

"What is that?"

"I'll tell you about it later. What am I saying, though, ashamed.
I'm only too lucky to have it. Things are bad, Russell. They were
when you left, of course, but they got worse and worse. Mr. Haynes
lost his job and they had to move, the Stonemans had to move, the
Palmers did. That's where the Stonemans lived. You remember
though, of course."

Another For Rent sign, on the door of the Stoneman house.
Empty now. He used to pal around with Greg Stoneman. Greg had
helped him build a roller plane once. It was basically a roller sled,
that they had put together out of a pair of two-by-fours and the
wheels of a roller skate. A bunch of kids had roller sleds. Newton
Avenue Hill was the coasting place. He and Greg Stoneman had
built plywood wings on theirs, and a tail and rudder. The old man
didn't like it about the plywood. It was a piece that had been under
the back porch, with the layers beginning to peel apart, but his
father said they should not have assumed the privilege of cutting it
up. His father chopped the wings off with a hatchet. They had
painted it that afternoon, with some red paint Mr. Stoneman had let
them use. Plywood was hard to chop, and the hatchet blade kept getting hung in it. But his father kept on, patient and steady. The paint
was still wet, and it smeared the hatchet, and it was like blood on the
hatchet blade. Greg Stoneman had once seen Lindbergh in person.

"Where did the Stonemans move, Mom? Do you know?"

"They're living downtown now. They found an apartment, that
wouldn't cost so much. They were talking about going down South
somewhere, and then they didn't. I have their new address somewhere. I think Mr. and Mrs. Haynes went to visit his people in
Scranton. The others, I really don't know. They just left. I thought
we were going to have to be the next ones. I managed to get on at the
Snow White, though. So we're still holding on."

"Was Pop working anytime?"

"The same as when you were here, Russell. He went to the office
every day."

They were at the house.

"Let's go on inside now, Russell. They'll want to see you. Karl and Wolfram and Calder, they're going to want to see you. Let's go on in now."

Somebody had pulled back the curtain at the front door. It was Wolfram. Peering out, and then his mouth opened. Then the front door banged, and Wolfram was running off the porch and across the yard.

"Russ!"

Wolfram stopped for long enough to yell back towards the house. He took off again, and charged into him.

"Russ!"

He knelt, and Wolfram was climbing over him. Struggling, squealing. Karl and Calder were there then. Karl was smiling. Calder didn't look exactly sure what had happened, but he looked as if he liked it. Calder was the baby. Four years old. Nearly five.

Wolfram kept talking. "When did you get here, Russ? We didn't know you were going to be here now. Come on, Russ, answer me."

"Be quiet, will you, so I can. Just this afternoon is—"

"What did you bring me? Did you bring me anything? When can I have it?"

"Brought you a kick in the pants, buddy. Turn around, so I can give it to you."

"That's not what I mean. What did you really bring me? You didn't have to, if you didn't it's all right, but if you did, tell me what it is. You hear me, Russ?"

His mother spoke to him. "Wolfram. Can you be quiet for ten seconds? Can you do that? He's glad to see you, Russell. We all are."

He went to work with her that night. She insisted that he ought not to, and yet he thought she wanted him along. She said that she herself had to get to work. She was already going to be late, and if she missed an entire shift she might lose the job entirely.

They had had supper, by that time. It was bread, with margarine on it, and boiled potatoes, and tea. Margarine never had looked good to him. This time it did, and it tasted good. He had only been eating candy bars and nickel pies on the way up from Florida, and he was hungry now for something cooked. The bread ran out, but he kept eating potatoes, salting them and letting the margarine melt into them. Wolfram watched him, and ate along with him.

Wolfram looked thin. All of them did.

"How much you weigh, buddy?"

"I forgot. How much, Mom?"

"Sixty-seven pounds."

"Is that enough, Russ? Is that what I'm supposed to weigh?"

"Sure. That's good."

About ten pounds too light.

"I believe you've gained some weight, Russell," she said. "And you look so nice and tanned."

"It's warm down there."

She got up. He did too, then, and got his jacket.

Wolfram was sulking. "You ought to stay here with us."

"I'll be back before long."

"You won't be back till Mom is. And that's always after twelve."

He had two pies in his jacket pocket, nickel raisin pies wrapped in waxed paper. He had got them at a filling station this morning, down in Winchester, Virginia. He had started to give them to Woolly and Karl and Calder earlier, and decided to wait. If they ate pies before supper they might not want anything else. That was what he had thought back then. They would have finished off a dozen pies, and their supper too. Sixty-seven pounds.

He handed them the pies. "You asked me if I brought you something? Look here."

"Oh. You did, didn't you?"

"Sure, buddy. I saved them special for you. And Karl and Calder." That was a damn lie. He only had them because he had got enough of that junk for a while. "Okay?"

"Yessir. Thanks a *lot*, Russ."

"You're welcome. What are you saying yessir for? I'm just your brother, buddy."

"Well—I just—. Wait a minute, Russ. I've got something for you."

"Wolfram, we've got to go, darling. Let's wait till we get back."

"Oh. Okay. I don't want to give this one to you anyway, Russ. If you'll wait, I'll give you a better one. Will you wait? It might be next week now. But it'll be better, if you do. It'll be a brand new one. A whole set."

"Wolfram. Russell, we've got to go." She had her coat on, and a scarf around her head. She had the package of lunch.

But when he started to the door with her, his shoe sole was flopping.

"Oh God. You can't walk with it like that."

He reached down, and ripped the sole off. "That'll fix it. Come on, Mom."

"No. You cannot walk over there, and back, with your foot on the ground. Just stay here, Russell, please. Don't make things any worse than they are."

Karl got up. "Mom? I know where some shoes are."

"Will you kindly tell me where any shoes can be in this house?"

"They're in the closet in there."

Karl got them. They were up on the shelf, in their box, with wooden shoe trees in them. Black ones. Shiny. Almost new.

". . . Oh. Yes. They were your father's formal shoes."

"See, Russ? A whole pair." Karl smiled at him. "One for the right foot, one for the left."

They were not too big for him. When he laced them tight, they were a good fit.

Metta had got him two pairs. Work shoes, and some for what she called off-duty. She required all her employees to have two pairs of shoes. He had not wanted to bring anything of hers with him, though, and he had only worn his old ones, when he left.

"You ought to button your jacket up, Russell. Wolfram. You and Calder. You're to do what Karl tells you, you hear me? Karl, they have to be in bed by nine o'clock. Let me see. No matches. The gas stove has to be kept turned off. Keep the doors locked. Don't answer the door if anybody knocks, no matter what. Don't burn more than one light bulb at a time."

Karl was patient. It looked as if he had heard it before.

As if she had said it before. He saw then that she was not saying it to tell Karl anything new. If she went through it every time, before she left, maybe it would keep them safe while she was gone.

He was sleepy. To bed by nine o'clock. Russell. Where had he slept last night. Down in Virginia somewhere. A town named Winchester. Russell. Four days and three nights. Miles and miles, cars and cars, highways and highways.

"Russell!"

He was looking at her. She had spoken to him. Three times. He had been dizzy or something, for a minute. It went away.

He felt better when they were outside. Cold air. March. In Florida it had been hot already. Several times he had seen flights of birds, dozens and hundreds each time, on their way north.

Getting dark already. His mother was walking fast. They both were.

They got there just before six. She had to see the foreman about punching in, since she was late. The foreman said Okay, when she told him she just hadn't been able to get here until now and she hoped it would be all right this one time. He was starting to get sore, at the foreman, when he heard the anxiety, the almost-servility, in her voice, but then he realized that nothing was the foreman's fault. The foreman's name was Vince. She called him Mister Vince. He asked her if there had been any trouble, and she assured him there hadn't. The foreman sounded like a decent man. She said then, This is my son. Vince grunted something, and told her then she had better go ahead and punch in.

He went along with her to the time clock, and then back to where the people were working. Vince did not call at them, or take them up on it. Evidently she would not need to explain why he was here, or ask permission for him to stay.

They were in a long room where women and girls, and a few old men, were busy at bundles of dirty clothes piled here and there on the floor along a table. A large pile of bundles had accumulated at her place. What she did, what the other pickers did, she separated the white things from the other things, and she checked to see if the pieces in each bundle tallied with the list for the bundle. Each list had a number and some letters penciled on the back of it. As she checked a bundle, she wrote the same number and letters with a laundry pen on the garments and sheets and such that she took out of the bundle. That was all there was to it, and it was complete hell. He would not have believed that dirty clothes could smell so bad. That there could be so many of them. That they could have as many different kinds of stains, smears, stickinesses.

She was in her third month here. She got twenty-seven cents an hour. When she first began, it was twenty-nine cents an hour. The pay had been cut last week, and somebody had said it was going to be cut again.

He sorted and checked with her. Before long, the pile of bundles was not so high at her place. More came in, but the two of them were keeping up. Vince the foreman came by once. Vince watched them for a minute, and said to him then, I guess you know you're doing this for free. He knew it. Vince went on down the room. The collector came along from time to time with a cart, and took the sorted clothes off the table. The collector was an old man, with glasses that had one lens cracked. The girl at the next pile down had yellow hair. She looked to be maybe seventeen or eighteen. He would be sixteen in July. She acted scared. Whenever Vince came by, she kept saying Yessir, as if she would do anything not to get him mad at her. They worked along. The room got too warm. His mother said it always did, about this time. The heat went up around eight o'clock and after that it would drop, and by the end of the shift, when the place closed for the night, the room would be cold again.

There was no special time to eat lunch. People ate as they got a chance to. What she had in the package was two bread-and-margarine sandwiches. She said she didn't have a brain in her head or she would have thought of making more. He didn't want any at all, on account of all the dirty clothes, but she insisted that he take one. His hands had the smell of the clothes. The place did not have anywhere for people to wash. There was a toilet, a single one for men and women both, and a water fountain, but no washbasin or tap he could have held his hands under. However, they could go outside to eat, out on a platform. It was cold out there, but they were in the open air.

It didn't take long to eat a sandwich. Then it was time to go back inside.

Not possible. He could not possibly spend four more hours in there.

What he would do, he would go on back to the house. She already knew he was pretty well done for. The kids were not supposed to be by themselves anyway.

It was nearly nine dollars that he had. He could give her that, and go on back.

If he was going to do that, he might as well have stayed in Florida.

"Russell? You're tired, darling. Why don't you slip on back home now? I'll be all right."

"That's okay. I'm not tired."

He saw on the platform, over by the wall, a copy of *Aviation Magazine*. Somebody had dropped it there, or thrown it away. The cover had a photograph of a Douglas DT-2. He recognized the plane—it was a biplane, a two-place Navy attack plane with pontoons and a liquid-cooled engine—but the magazine itself he had not seen before.

"Where are you going, Russell?"

"Over here a minute. Claim this magazine."

Pictures. Planes taking off, planes over carriers. Engines. Bombers. Seaplanes. Douglas. Hamilton-Standard Propellers. A plane dropping down, the nose high, high, onto a carrier deck, accepting the deck. Curtiss-Wright. Vought.

"Got me some reading material, Mom."

"I see you did."

The magazine had *August* on the cover. This was only March. It was a copy from last year. 1930. It was odd how it happened to be here. He would have it for when they got home tonight.

They had lived in this part of town, Newton Hill, when he was Calder's age. Later on, though, they were in another part of town. The houses were stucco then instead of wood, and they were farther apart than the ones in Newton Hill. None of them had front porches. Only concrete slabs at the doorways. Their house had a big initial K on the front door. There was a driveway for each house, two strips of concrete from the street, and a lawn sprinkler in front. His mother had a maid, and when Karl was born, a nurse for Karl. His father had a Reo car. It had a door to get in by, and a special small door behind that one, to slide a bag of golf clubs through. On Sundays, his father put the bag of clubs in, and drove out to the links for the afternoon.

His father was a member of a firm. It was Lupton-Lewis-Kaiser Realty. Wolfram was born by then, and they were living in another house, a very big one. This one was out from town. It was on a road instead of a street, Burgundy Road, in Burgundy Forest. When he asked where the trees were, since it was a Forest, his father said Are you attempting to be fresh with me, young man?

One winter they went to Florida, to visit Metta on her nut farm. Metta wanted him to spend the rest of the winter with her. When he looked at his mother, though, he saw he would not have to do that. He would get to go home with the rest of them. His mother said all of them should go back together, and Metta said Well really, and she assured his mother it was only an incidental suggestion.

Soon after they were home, his father went to Florida again, this time with Mr. Lewis, from the firm, and they set up a branch office in St. Petersburg. Mr. Lupton was not in the firm anymore. He had not wanted it to have a branch office, so they had made him leave. When his father and Mr. Lewis came back from that trip, in the fall, they had to move away from Burgundy Forest, to a house in town again. Something had happened in Florida, a boom, and Lewis-Kaiser had lost its money. The next spring it went out of business completely. His father did not have a car anymore, and went to work by streetcar. His father was a salesman now for Lupton Associates, and they moved back to Newton Hill. He was eleven years old.

His mother went to work too. She was a waitress, in the Trader Ho Restaurant. The Trader Ho was in the Monongahela Building, and in the old days, Lupton-Lewis-Kaiser had handled office leasing for the Monongahela. His father was sore at her when she started to work. He was sore almost all the time now. She said he had never liked the Newton Hill part of town. It was low-class.

The Trader Ho closed up, and so then she was out of work. There had been a crash, and places all through town were closing. His father went to the Lupton Associates offices every morning, but he never made any sales. He wrote to Metta, and she sent a check. He would not say how much it was for. In the mornings, he gave her a dollar bill and two quarters for the day's expenses, and at night he had her show him the list of what she had bought that day, so that he could see where his money was going. After two weeks, it was used up. The week after that, however, she found another job, this time in a diner.

"A diner. You're apparently determined on being a waitress. I expect a lunch wagon is slightly different from the Trader Ho. Especially this one. It happens to be a couple of Jews who own it. You didn't know that, I suppose."

"I don't *care* who owns it. It's a job, Helmut, it's a job. It is different from the Trader Ho, yes. It's in business and the Trader Ho has its doors locked. Don't look down on me, Helmut Kaiser, for working in a diner. What's wrong with that?"

"Nothing! Nothing is wrong with it. It might be interesting how much your compensation will be. How much that pair of Hebrews will let slip through their fingers."

"I can tell you how much the compensation will be. It will be twelve dollars a week. And tips in addition."

"And tips in addition. Well well."

That was in July. Later that month, his father did arrange a sale for Lupton Associates, and in August, another one. The business decline was not going to be serious after all. The upturn had already started.

No more sales, and in the fall his father began collecting rents and delivering eviction notices for the real estate company. He got a percentage of the rents when he could collect any, and he got thirty-five cents for each notice. Once he came home with his coat torn. There had been a scuffle with a tenant, about a rent collection. The tenant's wife, and son and two daughters, had joined in. "The scum," his father said. "The scum."

Back in the spring, Karl, sometimes Wolfram, had met him at the corner now and then, and warned him to wait a little before he went on home. "Pop's pretty mad at you, Russ. You better just wait, okay?"

At first, if he was with Greg Stoneman the two of them would go to Greg's house. If he was by himself, he would fool around somewhere. He had a Saturday job delivering groceries, so when he had a nickel or a dime he would pass some time in the Newton Hill drugstore. The drugstore had a newsstand, with magazines about flying. When he was broke, he went to the library, and read there about Montgolfier's heated-air balloon, and the Chanute and Langley aircraft, and the Wright brothers. One day when Karl warned him, he decided to go on to the house anyway. It turned out that nothing happened. When they got near the house he started getting cold feet, but he went on in. His father stood up, and his mother made a kind of sound. And then, his father only looked some other direction. And sat down again. And that was all there was to it.

At least most of the time that was all, but he still did not go to Greg's house or the drugstore to dodge his old man, even though he had to take a few punches sometimes. He more or less hated his father, but he was not especially afraid of him. And until the rent collection incident, that was how things went. Afterwards, there were more than a few punches, or attempts at more, and he learned to keep an arm across his face. It did not take any actual learning. A person's arm went up automatically. What his father wanted, he knew, was to be asked to quit, or else to be fought back against. His mother at first had remonstrated with him, until Russ had asked her not to. His father looked puzzled, off-balance, offended, when there was no asking or anything like it, or any remonstrating.

A time came when he was afraid of him after all. That was last October. It was the night when Wolfram ran to get Mr. Haynes, and when Mr. Haynes got there, his mother had just been shoved aside again and she was stumbling, trying not to fall down. Karl kept her from falling. Calder was howling. He had decided that now he would go ahead and hit back. He didn't weigh much, but he could use a chair, a shovel, anything. Then Mr. Haynes was there. Mr. Haynes only said "That's enough, Kaiser." To his father, and his father stopped. "You okay, young fellow?" He thought he was. His mouth was bleeding, but that was all. "I think you'll survive, don't you?" His mother had Calder quiet by then. She would get nervous later on, or anyhow she usually did after something like this, but for the time being things were calm. His father left the house. Mr. Haynes stayed a little longer, and then Mr. Haynes left too.

That was the particular thing that led to his going to Florida. Metta had written twice to say that he could work for her. They would have an easier time of it, she said, if there were one less for Brother to support for a few weeks or so, while correspondingly she could use the work he could do for her. She wrote once again, this time saying that while she could send him his ticket, that was the utmost she would be in a position to do. It had not occurred to him or his mother that she could do anything, but after that letter they began to think about what she was proposing. When she asked his father about it, his father was dignified. "I fail to see the harm in one member of my family visiting another member. I am a little surprised that you bother to consult me about it."

He kept his grocery-delivering pay from the next Saturday, and his mother added enough to it to make up his bus fare. Mrs. Haynes brought a box of sandwiches to the house. A while before bus time, Mr. Stoneman and Greg came by. Mr. Stoneman still had a car, and they were taking him to the station. At the station, Greg gave him a jacket. He didn't think Greg ought to do it. "Will you take it, stupid? Stop arguing?" So he took it. They were calling his bus then. He had the box of sandwiches, and the jacket, and another box that had pants and shirts in it. A lot of the people in the station had boxes and bundles and bags of things, instead of suitcases. He went to the gate, and showed his ticket, and went on through.

At Metta's, he liked the work fine. Besides the pecan orchard, she had a vegetable garden and ten pigs. She assigned him to work in the garden, and to help the handyman build a new pen, a brick one, for the pigs. When she said how high the walls were to be, the handyman told her that the pigs could get over it. She replied that she was paying him for work instead of advice, in case he wished to be paid. The handyman said Yes ma'am, yes ma'am, Miss Metta, I'll sure make it just the way you want it. They built it by the plan she had drawn. It was a good-looking wall when they finished. The pigs got over it easy. He had not known pigs could climb.

He found also that they were tame. At least for him they were, and part of his work came to be rounding them up when they got loose. They would grunt when he came near, and follow after him in a line. The handyman thought it was funny. Even Metta smiled once, or looked like she might be thinking about smiling, when she saw it. Each pig always took the same position in the line. If one of them tried to get a new position, the others would squeal and shove until it took its regular spot. Before long, the main part of his work was rounding them up. Metta finally ordered four more courses of brick put on the wall, and barbwire stretched along the top. She said they might have given her some assistance in the matter. Anybody could do mere physical labor. It would not have hurt them at all to make a suggestion about the construction of the wall. The new one kept the pigs in. The bricks, it occurred to him, and the mortar, and their labor, had cost more than some of the houses he saw along the road between her farm and the town of Palatka. When he said something of the kind to the handyman, the handyman said Sure. "They cost more than the shack I live in anyway."

The handyman, and himself, and all the others who worked for her, had to wear dark green dungarees and dark green shirts. On Sundays they had to wear white shirts. She did not care to have them smoking, especially cigarettes. She had forbidden him to use tobacco in any form. He never had, but she forbade it anyway. The town of Palatka had a movie theater, and she had also forbidden him to go to the Movies. When she learned that he and Karl and Woolly used to go sometimes, she looked him over. "Well! I can't see why Brother was writing to me so much for financial assistance, if there was enough for motion picture admissions." When she learned that he had seen a Jean Harlow movie, she said it was a difficult thing to believe. "A fifteen-year-old boy. Harlow. Harlot, if you ask me." It was *Hell's Angels* he had seen. Twice, and he had gone twice to see

Wings. Metta only allowed him to go to Palatka every two weeks, on Friday afternoons, and he needed to be back by five-thirty. He had no special wish to go at all, since it was a hot weedy little place and there were places he had found out on her ranch where he liked to be, but she insisted that he go, for recreation. He had to be in bed by nine o'clock, every night. Getting-up time was five a.m. Breakfast was at five-thirty. Fifteen minutes for breakfast and fifteen for lunch and twenty-five for supper.

She wanted him to go to the dentist in Palatka, and have the remnant of his broken tooth, a front tooth, taken out and a porcelain one or even, she said, a gold one, put in. The first time she said anything about it to him, she told him that she had made an appointment for him. He was well enough acquainted with her by then to know that the best way of dealing with her was to say plainly whether he would or would not do something. He told her he was not going to the dentist. That turned out to be the end of the matter. She opened her mouth and closed it two times, without saying anything, and the subject didn't come up again. The gap in his teeth was not an actual disfigurement. Even if it had been, he was unwilling to have anything done about it. He wanted the gap for a souvenir. In a way, it was a trophy. Also, he had figured out how to whistle again. For a time, the gap had prevented him from whistling.

The work was the easy part of being at her place. Long before he did leave, he was wanting to. Every week he wanted it more. February made four months he had been here. Early in March, he decided not to wait any longer. He would go home.

Metta said that since it was quite out of the question, she trusted he would not bring up the subject again. She had been paying him five dollars a month. In her account books, it was ten dollars, but she was putting five of it in the bank for him. He still had eighteen dollars of what he had been getting, and some change. That was enough for a bus ticket all the way. Then he realized that as soon as she found out he was gone, she would go to the Palatka bus stop, a grocery store and filling station, and if she got there before he had left, there would be an argument. It would not stop him from going. He just didn't want to be in an argument with her in a public place.

Or any other place. He went out to the pigpen, for a last look at the pigs. They seemed contented. He told them goodbye, but they didn't appear to be impressed. He would send the handyman a card from somewhere up the road. That was on one of the Friday afternoons he was supposed to use for recreation. He had forced himself to wait for Friday. Instead of going all the way in to Palatka, he began hitch-hiking as soon as he got to the highway, U.S. 17. When the first driver he thumbed stopped for him, and turned out besides to be going the whole way to Jacksonville, he knew he was in luck. By the time she realized he was gone, he would be long gone.

The first night he was home, Wolfram had said something about a present for him. Wolfram wanted him to wait for it, so that it would be a better one. During the second week he was back, Woolly kept going to the front door towards ten every morning, mail time. That week, nothing happened. The mailman went on past every morning.

The week after that, on Saturday morning, he was at the kitchen table, trying to wake up, wishing he did not need to just yet, wonder-ing if there would ever be a time now when he would not be buried under dirty clothes. He was working regular now at the laundry, six nights a week. His mother and Karl and Calder had gone to the grocery store, and he had needed to get up to watch after Wolfram. He knew the mailman was there when he heard Wolfram talking to somebody. Wolfram came back into the kitchen then, with a package. A very small one. Wolfram, not saying anything, watching him, gave it to him. It was addressed to Mr. Russell Kaiser.

The package had cards in it, with shiny colors. They were pictures of birds. Each one had the name of the bird in the lower left-hand corner. Bullfinch. Scarlet Tanager. Thrush.

"Don't you like it, Russ? I mean them?"

"Well sure. Sure I do."

Bluejay. Cardinal. Wren.

"Do you really like it? You're not just saying you do?"

"Come here, little dope. Certainly I like it." He put an arm around Wolfram's shoulders, and pulled him in. He noticed again how thin Wolfram was. Wolfram got tired quick, lately. "Did you think I wouldn't?"

"I thought you would, Russ. I knew you would. You know what I wanted to get for you? A model airplane. So you could help me build it."

"You wanted to get *me* one. So I could help *you* build it."

"Well, you know."

"I like these, Woolly. Better than a model plane. Thanks a lot, okay?"

"Sure. You're welcome, Russ."

Field lark. Robin.

Birds had hollow bones, for lightness. The wings were airfoils.

"You're welcome, Russ. You know how I got these? They're free. You send the coupon out of a box of oatmeal, see. And they send you back the pictures. And it doesn't cost anything at all. But that's not why I got it for you, Russ. I mean I didn't get it just because it was free."

"I know. I know you didn't."

"I'd get you the thing that cost the most of all, if I could. But all you do is send off for them. I sent off for one set already. But I wanted to get a new one for you, so that's why I said wait. So now we both have a set. Right?"

"That's right. We both do."

"I'll go get mine now, okay? We can spread them out on the table. Both sets."

Wolfram had a pencil, and a piece of paper, when he came back. He wrote something, and put the paper with the cards. The new ones. *From your brother Wolfram Kaiser. Very truly yours, Wolfram.*

He looked at it. And still did.

"Thanks a lot, buddy."

"Sure, Russ. Like I said, you're welcome."

He kept the cards. When Wolfram died, the next year, he threw them down in the alley. But then he went back out, in the rain this time, and gathered them up again. Eventually he had a son of his own, and named him Wolfram. There was war again by that time, and he was flying, a navigator. He was not sure for a few years if the second boy really was his own son, and he told one of the others on the crew, the only person he had come to be friends with, that it would serve him right if he had given somebody else's bastard his brother's name. But as the likeness firmed between his brother and the other one, and he had photographs to check his recollection against, it was clear that he was in fact the other boy's father. It disturbed him now and then when he thought of how close he had come to disclaiming him. And yet sometimes he almost would have. If only.

At the laundry, he had taken his mother's place. They arranged it with the foreman, Vince, the third night he went to work with her. It didn't matter to Vince which one of them worked, and so after the third night he went to the job by himself, and she stayed at home.

Most mornings, she looked for work herself. Up until January, she had been a waitress in the New Star Diner. Soon after that was when his father left. His father just didn't come home one night. The real estate company did not know where he might be. Neither the police nor any of the hospitals had any word about him. It looked as if a good many people were disappearing. In the paper there would be Personals ads, Anyone having information as to the whereabouts of. She had put one of those in the paper herself. She got the laundry job before too late. Now that he had taken that one, she kept looking for another waitress job, or any she could get.

In June, Karl finished the Seventh Grade. He himself would have finished the second year of high school, if he had gone on to school this year.

In July he was fired from the laundry job. Vince had given him a sort of promotion, to the folding and packaging room. He was handling clean clothes then, instead of dirty ones, and as soon as business got any better at all, he would get a pay raise. It got worse. When he was fired, Vince said he was only being laid off, but it amounted to the same thing. Three others were laid off at the same time.

Sometimes he got car-washing jobs, in garages. On Saturday nights, he worked in a bowling alley, setting pins. Greg Stoneman got that job for him. Greg was already working there. On Saturdays

the alley needed an extra pin boy, and Greg spoke to the manager
for him when the other extra boy got a wrist cracked by a flying pin
and had to quit.

The All For All Committee paid their rent one month, and Citi-
zens Self Help sent a box of groceries. The Red Cross came around
one morning, with some pails of garbage. Each one had only one
kind of garbage in it. Meat scraps, and vegetable leavings, and
partial slices of bread. It was what people had left on their plates in
restaurants. A program had been got up to save it and distribute it to
families in need. The Self Help box was one thing, but this was
something else. He told the woman to take the pails on away. She
said Will you tell one of your parents to step to the door, young man.
He told her again to take it on away. She was mad, but she left. She
was in a station wagon, a new one. You might know that people who
came around wanting to give you garbage would be in a big new
station wagon. Back inside the house, he wished he had not lost his
temper. The stuff had smelled good, and he was hungry, and
Wolfram and Karl and Calder were. If his mother had been there,
maybe she would have gone ahead and let it be brought in.

One night early in the fall, September, with Greg, he broke into a
grocery store. It was a chain store, a U-Bet, on Page Avenue. He was
surprised how easy it was. Greg had a drill, and a keyhole saw. Greg
drilled a hole through the door, just above the lock, and slid the
sawblade through, and they took turns using it until they had the
lock tripped out of the door. It was the door to a storage room, that
had cases of canned goods stacked along the walls. Greg struck a
match so they could see to read the labels, and they took a case of
corned beef, twenty-four cans to the case. Russ had bread, or flour
or something, also in mind. They took some rice instead, two cases of
one-pound boxes. And a case of chicken stew.

Greg had parked his father's car, a nine-year-old Essex, at the
back of the store. Having it that close was risky, but then the whole
business was risky, and this way they would not need to carry the
cases more than a few steps. They put them on the floor, in back.
Greg smiled at him. He was interested that Greg was so cool-headed.

The first couple of blocks, Greg drove with the lights off. Only one light was working anyway. Then, he pulled over, and stopped. He had to get out. The reaction from back at the U-Bet had reached him, and he had stomach cramps. He sat on the running board. Russ got out too. He didn't know just what to do, but sitting in the car was not it. Greg looked up once. Greg's forehead was damp. He put a hand on Greg's shoulder.

"Listen," Greg said. "I wasn't afraid, Russ. You hear? It wasn't because I was afraid."

"I know. Sure. I know it wasn't."

It came to him that it was because they were going against things they had thought should not be gone against. He had always assumed that ownership meant something. But he had also assumed that he meant something, that his mother and his brothers did.

After a time, Greg got up, and they got back in. The car would not start. Then it did, and they drove on. First by where Russ lived, since that was closer. Russ climbed over into the back, and divided the rice and the other food. He wanted Greg to come on inside and take it easy for a while.

"I'll be okay, Kaiser. I'll see you. Tomorrow, maybe."

The next week they made another U-Bet, and after that a Kroger. Both places were small ones. The big ones had night watchmen, and also, maybe, automatic alarms. There was no way of knowing ahead of time if the small ones had alarms too.

Once at a big Kroger place out in the Hazelwood section, a man knocked out a front window with a length of pipe. That was on a Saturday night. He was working in the bowling alley when it happened, but he heard afterwards that a crowd of people went on in before the police showed up. Nothing happened when the police did get there. They made the crowd come on out, and move away, and that was all. The newspaper only said that a business place in the Hazelwood neighborhood had been burglarized. It did not name the place as a grocery store. Greg's father said people would start getting ideas if the papers told all the cases of grocery stores being robbed. It was probably going on all over the country.

He had the impression that Mr. Stoneman knew what they were doing. He wondered, not very much though, how Mr. Stoneman felt

about it. Mr. Stoneman had a confused look sometimes. He saw the same look on almost everybody Mr. Stoneman's age. On the men anyway. Some of the women had a mean look. Some of them were scared. He figured his mother pretty well knew what he was doing. At least she must have known the bowling alley was not paying him in sacks of flour and cases of corned beef. Once when he was sitting at the kitchen table while she was cooking supper, she stopped, and turned and kissed him. She had not done that for years.

His mother had a mean look, and she had something to look mean about. Calder and Karl had both had colds. Karl had had to stay in from school. It was November now, wet and slushy. He himself got something of what they had had. With him it was worse. Fever, and for a stretch of days the fever kept him drowsy. He would doze off at the table, or anywhere he sat down, and find himself presently somewhere else. Where? They said that getting one off the ground was the easiest part. It could still be tricky. If you tried it before there was enough airspeed, you would stall. Drop, nose over, and break the propeller. And then you would be in trouble. Eventually he was well again. It seemed like a considerable time had gone by. Only three days. Karl and Calder were well. Not Wolfram. If Wolfram as much as sat up on the side of the bed, it exhausted him. Russ sat by his bed and fed him on the chance that that would save him some energy.

"Have I got the same thing you did, Russ?"

"Probably."

"Well, do you think I do?"

He watched him. "You do. It's the same thing, Woolly. Sure."

Wolfram relaxed. "Oh. Okay, then. If we had to be sick, at least we had the same thing, didn't we?"

Many of the times, he enjoyed getting the boxes and bags of food. It had come to be in his thoughts lately that his father would never under any circumstances have done things of that kind. That was all right. He could do the low-class things, and his father could have done the others. The two of them would have made a good team.

Maybe his father had left in order not to have to cheat, steal, break in. Maybe he had seen it coming that that was what he would have to do. Or else. And he had taken the or else. Everything he had tried for, and for a time, that short time, succeeded with, had been pulled out from under him. And in the end, the coat on his back was torn and ripped. Maybe it made sense, for his father to take the or else.

With Greg one night, Greg was dropping cans to him out of a window they had opened, and he was putting them in the car. Canned spaghetti a la tomato sauce. Sunny Italy brand. The window was high from the ground. They had needed to stand on the hood of the car to get the window opened. Greg had dropped three cans to him, when they heard a car on the side street. When it slowed, and turned, they knew it had turned in to the alley that led to the rear entrance here. The alley was paved, and it widened here into a paved areaway.

Greg climbed back out of the window. The car would not start. It was on a downslope, and with Greg at the wheel he was pushing it. Then the other car was there, big glaring headlights. Two men jumped out of it.

They had uniforms, gray ones, and police-style hats. They were not policemen. They were private guards. He had heard about them. This was about the tenth place he and Greg had been to. He had not supposed they could keep it up indefinitely, but he wished it could have been the police instead of private guards. These two had clubs, what looked to be clubs. It turned out they were lengths of rubber pipe. Greg had the car started, and Greg was yelling at him to get in. He couldn't, since one of the men was holding him and the other one was blackjacking him with the rubber stick. The one that had hold of him, Greg conked him with a can of spaghetti a la tomato sauce. The man let go, and stumbled away. Himself and Greg, Greg pulling at him, lifting him. An upstairs light went on in somebody's house. The car was moving. Greg was making a kind of noise, Are you hurt, Russ, Russ are you hurt, can you hear me, Russ, did they get you, did they. They were out of the alley. Open street. The other car could still catch up with them. Greg's would not go fast at all.

He found he was holding something. When he got his eyes focused, it was a pop bottle. From the dash compartment. They made good clubs. Maybe he could find one for Greg.

Before the other car caught up with them they had got to a tho-
roughfare, that had lights. People too, even as late as it was. The
other car did not follow them to where the lights were. It turned
down another street, and speeded up. And that was all they saw of it.

His ears felt full of water. When he gave his head a shake, they
cleared, and in a minute or so it would come back. He was probably
all right, though. Those two people had scared him, but maybe that
was all.

"I guess we drew a blank this time," Greg said.

They had. Greg had only dropped three cans. One of those had
been lost during the scuffling.

"Hell with it. We'll get you on home, Kaiser."

"You going home?"

"I guess so. I mean, sure. Anywhere else to go?"

He wondered what he had meant by asking.

A blank tonight. And there was not anything at the house for
tomorrow. Not even coffee.

"Listen—Greg." Because he knew now what he had meant. And
he was, now, finally, airborne.

"Greg? We can't go back like this."

"Hell we can't. Get you home, boy."

Climbing. And climbing still. Very high, and he and Greg were
small figures down there. Two of a great many, very small, busy,
back and forth.

"Listen. That place we were? Let's go back there."

"You out of your mind, Kaiser?"

Someday, now that he knew how, he might go still higher. For
now, no need to. He would come on back down now. He did, and he
was with Greg and himself again, in the car.

"I mean it. The way it is, see, that's the last thing they think we'll
do, now. They've already checked on that place. If they do come
back there, it won't be for two or three hours. We'll be gone, by that
time."

"Damn if I don't think you're serious."

"Come on. Okay?" Something was coming out of his ear. Flowing.

He would tell Greg to stop the car, and get out and go back by himself.

Then, Greg was slowing down. Had turned around, U-turn, without waiting to reach the corner. "Goddamn, boy. Here we go."

His right ear, the one away from Greg. Since it was that one, Greg would not notice anything until they were out of the car. And by that time, they would already be there.

Wild Honey

The truck had broken down back in the woods, and they had to get it fixed this afternoon. Jaxon's partner Bill Kirby was cutting timber with him, and Kirby was on his way to his own home to get a length of copper tubing to fix it with. Kirby was a good mechanic. Jaxon himself had come on to the house here instead of waiting around, to see if things were all right. He had stopped by a bee tree he knew of, but the coons had been there first, and all he got for his trouble was some bee stings.

Sarah was anxious about the truck. "Jaxon? Can you get it fixed?"

He ought to let her think he could. "Sure. Easy."

"I hope so. I just hope so."

"Put a little more of that soda on them stings, okay?"

"Well—if you really want me to. The thing is, it's just enough left now to make some bread for supper. Do you want me to?"

"Never mind. It's all right." Maybe they would stop burning by themselves afterwhile. "Any sugar?"

"Now what do you want sugar for?"

"I want it to eat. What else would I want it for?"

That was the reason he had stopped by the bee tree. The kids would have liked to have some wild honey. He would himself. Any kind of sweetening.

"It's not any here. I'm sorry, Jaxon, really and truly."

"Okay. That's all right. What else are we out of?"

"Jaxon, now it's nothing to joke about. Listen. I've got twenty-five cents. I been saving it, sort of, but I'll send Rafe to the store now, all right? He can get some soda, and some sugar too."

"You been holding out a whole quarter on me? How long you had that quarter?"

"Jaxon, I'm trying to tell you, it's not anything to joke about. Here. I'll put the rest of this soda on. And then later on I can send Rafe to the store."

"Have him buy a loaf of bread. I've got about fifty cents."

"He won't need to do that. I can make—"

"Have him buy a loaf. How many times have I got to say it?"

"All right. All right, he will, hear? You sit still now while I put this on. It won't take long."

He shouldn't have sounded off at her. He did sit still and she went ahead.

"Jaxon?"

And from her tone, he knew what was coming.

"Jaxon, you're bound to do something. If you'd just go on and get a job in the lumberyard with Carroll Yesbick, you wouldn't have to be doing all these things. Don't you see? You'd get paid every week, when anything broke *you* wouldn't lose anything, it wouldn't cost you anything. You'd even get paid for fixing it. I heard in the store the other day that he wants somebody to work for him. I didn't ask, now, I didn't say a word. I just heard somebody say it. He hasn't got anybody to replace Dan Johnson yet. And maybe you wouldn't have to work right there in the lumberyard. Maybe Carroll Yesbick would let you—I mean, maybe you could still be working out in the woods. On one of the cutting gangs."

He got up. "Let me tell you something, Sarah. Let's don't go through this again." He was not talking loud. "Carroll Yesbick won't be letting me do anything. Or not do anything. I'm not having anything to do with the son of a bitch, you know that? Neither is Kirby. Neither is anybody else that's got the idiot notion he's worth a damn. I'm not working for Yesbick. Any time. For any kind of pay. Will you hush about it now? Going on at somebody, it gets on a person's nerves."

"It does, does it? What do you expect me to put on the table for supper this evening, tell me that? The same old thing, I suppose. What are you going to do when school starts, Jaxon Chancellor? School takes in again next month, have you thought of that?"

"I know when school takes in."

"Then what are you going to do? Leslie needs—" And now she was close to tears. "She's too big to go barefooted to *school*, Jaxon. She's twelve now, she asked me the other day if we could get her a pair of shoes maybe. They don't have to be nice ones, Jaxon. Just so she can have *some*."

"She'll have some shoes."

"How? How? And Nora needs things too. They both do. Rafe does."

"Right now, I don't know. I'll have to tell you that. You know I don't. But she will have some."

"But how? Jaxon, *please*."

He waited a little. "Sarah. I got to get on back now."

She didn't say anything.

He waited. He thought maybe she might go ahead in a minute and give him an answer.

Before she did, Rafe came running in.

"You still here? Daddy, you still here?"

"What's the matter with you, boy?"

Rafe was seven years old this year.

"I thought you'd gone already without letting me know."

"I got to check things out with you, boy?" Jaxon smiled at him. "Before I do something?"

Rafe became shy. "No sir. I don't guess so."

Jaxon put an arm along his shoulders. "Yes, I do. Come here, Rounder. Don't you know I wouldn't go off without you and me saying so long first?"

Rafe stood close against him. "Yessir. I do. I just wanted to make sure."

"Listen, Rafe. How about going to the store for your mother, all right?"

"Yessir. Sure. What do I have to get?"

Then Sarah was telling him to walk across the bridge with him, and telling Rafe to be careful on it coming back when he would be by himself. It was only a footbridge, but it had a handrail, and Rafe could get across on it all right, but she made him promise to hold the handrail anyway.

Yesbick was a timber operator. He owned power saws and trucks and tractors, a sawmill and planing mill and lumberyard, a side business in hardware, paint, and building supplies. He sold the pine his crews cut to the big furniture mills in High Point, North Carolina, to plywood plants in Richmond and Knoxville, to the paper mill in Covington. Most of the people around the Benediction community worked for him. A good many of them lived in houses that belonged to him, and the rent came out of their pay before they were paid. He had put up a double row of dwellings, one room wide and three rooms long, back of his main sawmill, and it was understood that he wanted the people working for him to live in them. He owned various tracts of land, and he had leased timber rights all through Benediction County and the next one over. The region around Skater's Creek, over in the next county, only had weeds and thorns and gullies now. He had had all the trees there cut down, even though by the law he could only cut some of them, and that section had changed into wasteland. When Benediction County was paving some of its roads after the war, it built two new ones, and paved them, to points that had been hard to get into and where he had timber cutting going. This past summer, surveying had started for a new main highway through here. The Benediction section was in a pocket to itself, not on the shortest or easiest route for the new road, but the new one would swing down to Benediction and then north again. His trucks would make better time then, with less wear and tear than they could now.

That was all very well, but it didn't much interest Jaxon. He went his way. For his logging he had a secondhand truck, six years old now, and some saws and chains and axes. Bill Kirby had some saws, and he was good at repairing the truck. Each of them owned a few acres, and although the land was too steep for anything besides timber, they did own it.

Jaxon's timber, and also Kirby's, was mostly oak and cedar. The town of Liberty, fourteen miles away, had a small furniture shop that specialized in handmade chests and tables, and it wanted hardwoods instead of pine and poplar. Outside Roanoke, there was a veneering plant that when it needed an extra number of walnut logs, bought from them. Between the veneering plant and the furniture shop, he and Kirby had a market. With Kirby, he could have cut and hauled half as much again as he actually did, if he had had some place to sell it. As things were, his income was a now-and-then matter. But the alternatives were to pick up and move away, or if he stayed here, go to work for Yesbick. Many people already had left. In the section generally, there were only five or six small-time loggers now, jackleggers, besides himself and Kirby. He was staying. And he was going to keep on working for himself.

He got back to the truck a few minutes before Bill Kirby did. Kirby brought the copper tubing he had gone after. The oil line to the engine had started leaking. The truck was already loaded, with walnut logs, and they had been on their way out of the woods to Roanoke and the veneering mill, when the oil pressure dropped and the engine began overheating. Kirby stopped and located the trouble.

The repairing was simple. It involved cutting the pipe and fitting a new piece in and securing it with banding clamps. They already had oil to replace what had leaked out, since they kept an extra gallon. The engine used a lot of oil. And with the line mended and new oil in, they could get under way again.

"Think we ought to try it?" Kirby said.

It was a question. They would need to do some tall driving. The office at the veneering plant closed at five-thirty, and they couldn't get paid unless they got there before it closed. It was after four now. A fifty-mile trip, with a big hill to get over, Jack's Mountain, and an overloaded truck. Both rear tires were smooth. The front tires were slick. They would be squeezing the truck and the engine for maybe more than it could give. Kirby wanted him to do the deciding. And if he did, and they ruined the truck, that meant the responsibility would be on him.

"Let's roll. Not getting anywhere staying here."

Kirby smiled. "That's what I wanted you to say. Couldn't work myself up to it, I guess. Just hope we'll make it, though."

"Let's go. We'll make it."

They checked the load again. They had the logs lengthways on the truck, with chains over the top, and the ends of the chains hooked to the sides, and extra stakes along the sides. It looked secure. They got in.

They were at the veneering mill before the office closed, and they got the logs unloaded and weighed in. The foreman gave them a purchase voucher, and they went to the office. A bonanza. The voucher read $165.00, and that came to $82.50 for each of them. Shoes. Groceries. Candy. Soap. New pants and a shirt for Rafe. Kirby's youngest kid was sick. He had a two-year-old girl, and a boy about Rafe's age. The doctor wouldn't see her without cash money. Kirby's wife bathed their kid's eyes with warm water and boric acid, but that only helped for a few hours at a time. Now they could carry her to the doctor. Eighty-two dollars and fifty cents.

They had a better bonanza than they thought. Or they would have one, since the manager in the veneering office gave them another order for logs while they were there. Another truckload. They could bring it in any day this week. Tomorrow, or the day after, or any day.

It would need to be the day after, since it would take that long to get another load cut and delivered. On the strength of the new order, when they went on into Roanoke they bought two new tires at the Acme Tire Market, and a recap for a spare. Kirby also got new spark plugs and a set of points for his car. He had an old Plymouth, but he didn't use it any more than he had to. Usually he walked out to the woods. Since he would be taking his kid to Liberty tomorrow, to the doctor, he wanted his car to be in shape.

From the Acme, they went to a Kroger store and loaded up. Flour, oatmeal, canned milk, sugar and dried beans and sidemeat and hamburger meat. Supplies were cheaper here than at Hube's Store, out in Benediction. The people here also acted like they wanted to sell the stuff, like that was the reason they had the store. At Hube's you almost needed a membership ticket to buy anything. Jaxon got a

ten-pound bag of sugar. It was sugar he had been wanting, and he
got candy besides, chocolate and licorice and cinnamon rocks,
although most of that would be for the children. Kirby got a bottle of
lotion for his wife. She liked those things when he could get any for
her. "This here cosmetic crap," Kirby said, and he made it clear that
he personally, being practical-minded, didn't put any stock in it.
Jaxon was interested. He got three bottles of lotion, small ones, for
Sarah and Leslie and Nora. Leslie would have new shoes now, for
school. And Nora would.

It was dark by the time they started home. They only had a few
dollars left. That was all right. Day after tomorrow they would get
paid again. They were used to having to spend most of their money.
All of it, but this time they had come out ahead. The truck rolled
along. Engine running cool, the headlights steady and bright, the
moonlight gray and quiet over the fields. Heavy dew. In the headlights, grass by the road glittered from the dew.

Neither one of them had had any supper. They had overlooked
getting any. That was okay. He would get supper when he got to the
house. Half an hour now, forty-five minutes. He pushed down on the
gas pedal. The engine answered, and Kirby sort of laughed. "Want
to get home, don't you, buddy?"

They got another load cut the next day, on Kirby's land this time,
and got it loaded the following morning. Another fifty-mile trip, but
this time they could go slow and still be back before the turn of the
afternoon. However, on the way up Jack's Mountain they had a
blowout. A rear tire, the right rear. One of the new tires. The old rear
ones were on the front wheels now. Jaxon was driving. The truck
lurched. He kept it under control. A blowout in a front tire was the
bad kind for steering. He was stopping, and pulling over, when the
truck lurched again, and the whole rear end of it dropped. It kept
moving, scraping and grinding, for long enough to be off the pavement, and that was as far as it would go.

When they got out, they found that the rear axle was broken in
two. What with the blowout, and the load of logs, the axle had
snapped. Tire and tube gone, new tire, and also the right wheel

ruined, part of the rim flattened. Oil was flowing out over the differential casing and spreading over the ground. The differential was pulled apart. The more they looked, the worse things got. Probably a bearing shot, in that wheel. The drive shaft probably bent.

He didn't want to leave the truck. But it was out here on the mountain, loaded and busted.

They were six miles now from Benediction. Four miles from Kirby's house. Jaxon's idea was for them to walk back to Kirby's and get his car, and get on over the mountain then and to the veneering mill. They would see about arranging there for one of the mill's trucks to be sent out to here, and they would transfer the logs to it. He didn't know anybody at the mill, but it was worth trying.

Kirby had another idea. A man he knew in Roanoke, Owen Marron, used to be his nearest neighbor. Jaxon knew him slightly, since Marron used to be a jackleg logger like themselves when he lived here. He had moved to Roanoke last summer, after he got fired from Yesbick's. Kirby's wife and Mrs. Marron wrote to each other now and then, and Kirby knew Marron's address. The point was that Marron had a truck, and he would let them use it. They could pay him for it. He might even come along with them and help them change the load from their truck. That would save them some time. They would need to pay him something for his work besides something for using his truck, but Marron wouldn't want anything out of reason.

Jaxon decided to go along with this. They had to walk all the four miles to Kirby's house. It was after two o'clock when they got there. They ate some dinner at his house. They didn't want anything, but since Jaxon was company, Mrs. Kirby insisted on doing something that would look like making him welcome. She set plates, and fixed eggs and pancakes for them. By the time they had finished eating, Jaxon was glad she had insisted. With a hot dinner, he began to think they would get the situation dealt with after all.

When Mrs. Kirby heard they were going to see Marron, she went to a shelf, and took down a coffee can, and opened it.

"You carry Sadie Marron some of these crocus bulbs, Bill. She went and left all her flowers and plants when they moved, and she said the last letter I got she missed them. And that was back in the summer. Mr. Chancellor, does your wife pay much mind to flowers? Here." She found a paper bag, and put some bulbs in it. "You carry her these. And you tell her now, in case she might not know, the way you do crocus bulbs, you plant them in the fall. Any day along about now would be all right. And the next spring, is when they come up. I've seen it still snow on the ground and there the little things are, peeping their heads out."

Kirby got up. "Mildred, you talk a person's head off. Me and Jaxon can't hang around here."

"Bill Kirby, you can hush now." She got his jacket for him, and Jaxon's, and she was telling Jaxon to come back when he could and plan to stay longer, and bring his family when he could.

He was sorry to leave this house. This seemed odd to him. The other times he had been here he would have stayed longer if there had been time, but there had not been this unwillingness to go.

Kirby drove fast. They were in Roanoke by four o'clock, but they didn't know the city, and it took them another half hour to find Marron's house. The streets in that part of town didn't have any pavement, or sidewalks. The houses were cheap-looking, close to the street and close together. Jaxon had only know Marron slightly, but he hadn't figured Marron would be living in a house like one of these. He asked Kirby where Marron worked.

"Got on at the pants factory here in town. Did something in the shipping part, what my wife said."

When they got to Marron's address, the house was empty. The front door had a padlock on it. The windows didn't have any curtains or shades. The rooms didn't have any furniture. Some of the windowglass was broken out.

They sat in the car. "Something must happened to Owen," Kirby said.

Kids with sores on their faces were standing in some of the yards. Not playing, exactly. Just hanging around.

At the house to the left of Marron's, a woman was looking out a front window. She came out onto the porch and called at them.

"You folks trying to find somebody or something?"

"Maybe she knows," Kirby said. He got out of the car, but when he did, she moved back to the door. He stopped, and only called at her, to ask if she knew of an Owen Marron that used to live here.

Marron had moved, last month. She thought they had gone to Bluefield, but she didn't know for sure. "Mr. Marron got out of work, see, and from what she said, I gathered that's where they meant to go. Lord, I don't think that poor thing knew, though, where they could go. Why? You all want to see him or something?"

"Wanted to see him about his truck," Kirby said.

"He didn't have any truck, mister. Now he *did* have one, you're right about that, used to park it just where you all are now, but that was back when they were first living here. Seems to me he sold it or something. I couldn't say for sure, but I know he didn't have no truck when they left here."

Marron didn't used to live in a house like this one. Nothing like this one. When people moved, it looked like they went to something worse. When they started running, that was it. Rafe. What if Rafe was in a yard like one of these. Sores on his face. Leslie and Nora. God.

"Want some crocus bulbs?" Kirby said.

"Do what?"

"I say you want some crocus bulbs?"

"Don't believe I do today, thank you." She was going back inside then. Closing the door.

"Real good ones," Kirby said. He was talking to himself. "Better take some, while you got a chance. Oh Jesus. He's already moved. Don't have a truck even if he did live here." He got back in the car. "My sweet Jesus." In a minute, he started the engine.

"Let's stick around here a while," Jaxon said.

"Here? Let's get out of here, man. Quick as we can."

In the Liberty Cafe, Jaxon asked the waitress for another cup of coffee. He didn't need to get any more, since three or four other people were at the counter only loafing, not buying anything, and he could be one of them. But some more coffee would be something to do.

He had been to the bank this afternoon. To try and make a loan from the Liberty National Bank. That was his last try, he knew before he made it, and now that he had, he was glad to have it out of the way. A mortgage, on the sixty acres he owned. Nothing came of it. The man in the bank asked him how much land he had, and where it was situated. Then he sort of smiled. I don't think we'd be interested in that, Jaxon. At first, the man said Mr. Chancellor. Then just Chancellor and then just Jaxon. When he was leaving, two of the clerks that worked in the bank looked at him, and looked at each other. They had the same kind of little smile the man in the office used.

And he had time now to sit around. He could not remember when he had been so free and easy.

Kirby had a job outside town, two miles north. He was working in a filling station, a little place that somebody kin to his wife owned. He was good with cars and trucks, and he started there yesterday. Not that he did anything in particular with cars and trucks. It was only a filling station, and he pumped gas and tried to find things to make himself handy at. Kirby had looked ashamed, telling him. What bothered Kirby was that they could possibly have sold his Plymouth and arranged that way to get the truck running. Instead, Kirby got the filling station job, and he had to have the car to get to and from work.

"It's just that it looks like I'm running out on you," Kirby said. "That is, I do have a car, more or less of one, and Jesus, man. You ain't got nothing."

So he told Kirby not to feel that way about it, since there was no reason to. He said it because it was what Kirby wanted him to say, but as soon as he had, it was also what he meant. Kirby didn't look ashamed anymore and he looked to be feeling better.

That was yesterday. Day before yesterday was the time they were in Roanoke. Coming back, they saw the veneering mill foreman about using one of the mill trucks. The foreman would not hear of it. If they couldn't get an order delivered, that was too bad. Excuse me, boys, I've got to get busy now. That night, they went to Dorn's Garage to try to get the parts they needed, but Earl Dorn said he couldn't be selling to them on credit. Earl Dorn was Yesbick's brother-in-law. They went to a junkyard in Liberty, but the junkyard owner took the same position as Earl Dorn. They had a little over six dollars between them. They could get one part, but one would not be any good without all the others. Wheel, driveshaft, differential. Tires, bearing, differential case. Bearing, differential, wheel. The next morning, which was now yesterday morning, the Road Department had the truck towed to the county vehicle yard. They owed the county a fine now for the towing.

He didn't need to be thinking anymore, though, about driveshaft, bearing, tire. That was over with.

Afterwhile, he left the cafe. He would need to see about getting back to Benediction. It was a twelve-mile trip from here.

He understood now why he hadn't wanted to leave places, the past few days. It was to postpone having to see Yesbick. A delay might give time for something to happen. For things to have a chance to shift, and happen a different way. If they were let alone, and given just a little more time, they might do that.

Although in the first place he was taking for granted that he could get on at Yesbick's at all. Yesbick was just as likely to tell him nothing doing, as to hire him. A lot of people did work for him, but then a lot didn't.

He had two dollars and some change now. At the house, there was a fair supply of groceries. From the buying he had done the other night. That long time ago. Sarah had got a few more things the next day, at Hube's. It was a treat for her to get to go to a store. There was enough in the house for three or four days ahead. It was not necessary to see Yesbick today. He could wait another full day, and another one after that.

No. No more putting off. And then, when it was done, to get home.

"You want to see me about something, Chancellor?" Yesbick said. "Not looking for a job by any chance, are you?"

"It's what I'm doing."

He had not realized how big the lumberyard was. Long sheds, a brick and concrete building for the power saws and shapers and

planers, an unloading dock, another one up at the far end for the
worked lumber to be loaded and hauled away. A sawdust pile. A
long hill of sawdust. A row of trucks. Stake body trucks, flatbeds,
pickup trucks. Two or three sedans. The place was quiet now. End of
the day, and working hours were over. They were standing now outside the office. Yesbick had been getting ready to leave.

"What you're doing, huh," Yesbick said. "Well, let's see now.
Fact is, I'm not actually taking on anybody right at the present
time."

Jaxon was looking at a drinker's face. Yesbick was a heavy man.
He must have been a bruiser once. There was probably a way to ask
for a job. To tell the man how much you had to have one, how much
you'd appreciate it if he could see a way.

Yesbick looked mad about something. Dissatisfied, more than
mad. It looked like he couldn't get away from being dissatisfied.

"But I guess I could find something for you to do," Yesbick said.
"I know I don't need anybody out at the logging, though. Think you
could help out around the yard here? Never worked much with
machinery, did you?"

"Swinging an axe. Snaking logs out."

He remembered something Kirby had told him once. That
Marron had said. Yesbick got some pleasure out of hiring jackleggers. Yesbick would hire them ahead of the others, but he would
never, even when a timber crew was short-handed, put them on a
timber crew.

"Uh. Could use a man that knows equipment. Maintenance. Or I
guess I could."

It sounded like Yesbick was going to hire him. For if not, he
wouldn't be talking about it. He was talking like he might not, but
that was only for principle. It was all over, then. It was finished.

"Well, I don't know, though. We could try you out on it, see how
you work out. When you thinking about starting? Think you could
start in the morning?"

It didn't have to be all over. There was still time to tell the man he
had only been asking to be asking. "Tomorrow morning? Sure."

Yesbick looked at him. "Understand you had a little accident with your truck. Sorry to hear about that."

Yesbick must have heard about it from his brother-in-law. Dorn.

"You live over on Benediction Run, don't you? Guess you might as well stay on there, then. Right at the start anyway."

Yesbick was telling him where it was okay for him to live.

His grandfather's father had put up the first dwelling on that location. It was a cabin, and it was still standing, with more rooms and a porch added on.

He had not thought of not staying there.

What Yesbick might be thinking of was the row of little houses over beyond the sawdust pile.

Yesbick was looking at him. "Well? You want to go to work here, Chancellor? Or don't you? Don't have all day."

He knew what he needed to say. There was a way to ask, all right. And the tone of voice to say it in. He did it he wanted the job.

The woman in Roanoke had called Mrs. Marron that poor thing. He thought of the kids in those yards.

Things cost so much. The cost that they had.

The way it stood, though, the thing he was only just now finding out, maybe even now not completely, was that he had the price of it. He could meet the cost.

Yes I do. Don't you know I wouldn't go off without you and me saying so long first.

Nobody would be calling Sarah that poor thing. Not while he could stand between her and them.

"Well, Chancellor? You want the job or don't you?"

"Yessir. Yessir, I sure do, Mr. Yesbick. Thank you too."

Yesbick could do what he could do. And could not do what he could not do.

"Don't thank me, son. Thank the good Lord it's jobs for anybody to work at. You be here tomorrow morning, then. Seven o'clock's the time. Might as well make it a quarter till, while you're at it."

The Feast of Crispian

For a while, Kiwi had been planning to put his shoes on. He had got as far as getting his trousers on, and then he had started thinking of something else. And doped off then to something else still. Not thinking of anything much now. Nine-thirty almost, and still he was not in motion.

For something to do, he studied his feet. It was the left one that had got burned the worst. At Trinidad last summer, the tanker he was on got hit, just after they started home, and he had to hop through some hot oil. It must have been the left one he was hopping on. Sometimes he tried to remember which one, to get it straight once for all, but so far he had not been able to. At the time it happened, there was too much happening. People yelling and rushing, the oil just short of being on fire, people, himself one, sliding around in it. They had only just left port, the city of Trinidad was still in sight, when they got hit. He was not doing any hopping on either foot, the next two months. French-fried feet. Oil smoking, people trying not to slip and fall in it, falling anyway. French-fried people. It felt like something shameful, afterwards. Fellows he knew that had to have crutches, they didn't want to go out in public. He had not wanted to himself.

Denise, behind him, turned over and made a murmuring sound. She always slept later than he did.

She was saying something again. Anyway making sounds. She said once that he had been talking in his sleep one afternoon, and he had said her own name. She sounded now like something was bothering her. While he watched her, though, she became quiet.

Her hair was tangled. Denise was sharp, once she got her face fixed and her hair calmed down, but it took her a while to get it done.

Denise Houston.

He put a hand, carefully, along her face. It didn't wake her up. Her face only relaxed. And the muscles in her neck did.

She was an actress. She had told him that the first night he met her, downstairs in the bar of this New Yorker Hotel.

"You wouldn't have heard of me, though," she said, that night. "I only had walk-on parts . . . Now I have lay-down parts." They were upstairs by then, and he had asked her if she was really an actress. She was grumpy at first, that night.

"What were you in?"

"Oh—*The Blue Mirror. High Wide and Handsome. Bamboo.* Ever hear of those?"

"Sure. I've been to see *Bamboo.* I've been to a lot of plays."

"Oh. We keep up with the theater."

"Don't get excited. Plenty of people go to plays . . . I shipped with a fellow was in *The Blue Mirror.*"

That got her a little more interested. "Who?"

He told her the man's name, and it turned out she knew him. "Small world." But she didn't sound so grumpy anymore, and before long, things were fairly cheerful. They had had several drinks by that time, besides, or anyway he had, and there was not any shaking in his voice anymore. There had not been any excessive amount anyway, since he had been off the ship for nearly a week already, and she had pretended not to notice what there was of it, but by then there was not any. The man he had shipped with that had been in the play with her—his name was Jack McAuley and people called him Jack Mac and he had been a deck man, an Ordinary—had been killed down there at Trinidad. He had only got his feet burned, and Jack Mac had been killed. He didn't tell her about that. Maybe she had known him well, and it would depress her if she heard about it.

To get the rest of his clothes on. Get washed up.

Her eyes opened. Then she was looking at him. "Doing up so early? Time is it, Kiwi?"

"Nine-thirty."

She smiled. "Were you looking at me any time this morning?"

"A minute ago I was. Why?"

"I dreamed you were. I was dreaming you said you were leaving, and then you were looking at me, and I realized I'd only been dreaming that you . . . Oh. You did say it, didn't you?"

"Yes. Yes I did, Denise."

"Oh. You did, didn't you."

"We talked about it, Denise."

"Of course we did. Sometimes I think I must be a moron, the way I forget things. Except I just wish you didn't have to leave. I didn't want to remember that."

"I wish I didn't have to either, Denise."

He was going to get another ship. It would probably be this morning. He was going to the union hall, and sign on the first tanker that wanted a bosun. He had been ashore for a month now. Thirty days, and after thirty days, seamen automatically got drafted.

"I have it to do, though, Denise."

One way or the other, he had it to do. Whether he let himself be drafted, whether he got a ship. It was going to be a ship. He was twenty-eight years old, and he had been shipping out since he was eighteen, longer than that, and that was what he was going to keep on doing.

"Didn't you say once you've been shipping out eleven years, Luks?"

"About that long."

"I was still in grade school eleven years ago. Out in Cincinnati, Ohio." Her voice became tough. "I'm one of them middlewesterners, sport. So don't get fresh, you know what I mean?" She giggled.

"Let's hear you talk like a bosun."

"Belay that rigging, Mate. Please. Is that how you sound?"

"Not exactly. I don't generally say please. In fact, I practically never tell them bastards please."

"Who? You mean your fellow crew members, don't you?"

"Yeah. That's exactly who I mean."

A bosun. Tankers. Most of the people he knew, Hughes for example, the ones it seemed like it made any difference knowing, they had rather go on tankers. When he got to the union hall, the *Richmond* might be in again. That was the ship he had got off last month, and if it was in, he would locate Hughes. Hughes had stayed on, and if he was still on, he would sign on again himself.

Last month. It was not all of a month he had known her.

It still felt surprising that he had got to know her. That she hadn't brushed him off the first time he spoke to her. That was downstairs, in one of the bars. He was about as beat up when he got off the *Richmond* as anybody could get. Half the people he saw looked like they needed to be slammed into. He couldn't stand it for anybody to come up to him and start saying anything, his own voice was shaking so bad he had to study in advance what he wanted to say and even then it was most of the time just as bad. The bartender had asked him what nationality he was. He had intended to say American, any of your damn business? What came out was only sounds, stammers, that shaped up into "I'm a seaman," and the bartender said I figured it was one of them countries over there. He knew what was wrong. He had seen other people in the same situation. It went by the name fatigue. Convoy shock. But knowing the name of it didn't mean much. He got off the *Richmond*. Hughes was insisting on it, and he might have got off anyway. That was how it was, when he met her, and most women wouldn't have wasted their time.

If only he didn't have to leave.

Right. Sure thing. You bet. He did anyway.

He stood up then, rubbed a thumb along his jaw. Scrape some of it off. Shower.

This hotel had elaborate heads. A washbasin shaped like a sea shell. A glass door on the shower compartment with carvings of dolphins and waves.

When he came back, she had coffee getting ready in the kitchenette. He got his seabag out of the closet. It was already nearly filled, since he had only taken some things out of the top. He would not need to use up much time now for packing. He opened a bureau drawer. A pint of brandy lay between two shirts. Hennessey.

"Look what I found, Denise. Want some?"

"Not before breakfast, Luks. Good heavens."

"Some in your coffee."

"Not even with coffee."

She didn't care for liquor. Whenever there had been any drinks, she hadn't much more than sipped at hers. He left the bottle unopened, and put it in the seabag, and put the two shirts on top of it.

Denise glanced at herself in the mirror. "My sweet mercy."

"I've seen worse."

"Not much worse. Mercy." She took her hairbrush from the bureau, and went on into the bathroom.

A sweater on top of the two shirts. Then his shaving kit, and a couple of towels. With that, the bag was filled. He drew the line tight through the grommets and tied the line. The packing was finished.

Suitcases. He had had some good ones once, a matched pair, dark brown genuine leather. His ship had been bombed, and that was the end of them.

London was where he had been at that time. London was getting it bad, over and over. The docks there had had wooden blocks for paving and the blocks were on fire. One of the warehouses had sugar, and the sugar melted and ran out over the street and caught fire, and the worse all that racket and burning got, the more it smelled like caramel.

Got his shoes on then, with the laces slack so as to keep the healed burns from starting to itch. They would anytime he gave them a chance. A necktie. Then his coat. This suit was nearly new. Dark blue flannel, from Brooks Brothers, one he had got last fall when he got out of the hospital.

His wallet was in the breast pocket of the coat. American Express checks, and some cash. He would see her again today, or anyway before the ship went, and he could have the checks cashed by that time. He already knew she was sort of broke. It had been several weeks since she had had a part in any play. Maybe they shouldn't have stayed in this hotel. She had an apartment, and the hotel was expensive. Even now, after two years of it, he was not used to making good money. It was like not being actually used to her, to having it make any special difference to anybody whether he stayed home or left.

Some more coffee. The pot still had plenty. Still hot.

She came back while he was drinking it, and he poured a cup for her. She looked good now. Her hair was so black it shimmered. Two or three times he had brushed it for her. She had also put some perfume on. Maybe it was cologne.

She regarded him. "You have good presence, Luks. Actors have it sometimes. You're heavy, and still you—." She sat down. "Oh well."

"You better belay that rigging, Mate. Please."

"I know. I know. I don't *want* to be all dramatic about it." She stood up again. She was smiling.

"Listen. I wish you'd stay here for about two hours, Denise. All right? I'll call you here as soon as I know what I'm going to be doing. And when, and all that. Will you?"

"I'll be right here, Luks."

He swung the seabag up onto his shoulder. The movement took him across the ribs, and he waited until that went away. He had got a rib cracked, at Trinidad. His hands cut, in the same general uproar.

"We had a good time, didn't we, Denise?"

"Didn't we, though? Didn't we just."

He drew her close, with his free arm, and she lay against him. "You know I would stay if I could. You know that, don't you?"

"Yes. I do, of course I do."

"And we'll have a good time again. Right?"

"Won't we, though? Won't we?"

"Sure we will. I'll b-b---" he had to stop for a minute, to plan ahead what to say.

"What is it, Kiwi? I heard the b-b- part. What is it, darling?"

"I'll be back." It worked, this time. "Okay? I'll be back, you hear?" Steady, every word.

The Union Hall, National Maritime CIO, was on 17th Street. The ten-thirty call was over when he got there, and people were crowding through the front door and out to the street. He went on in. There would be another call at eleven.

The callboard, that hung from the ceiling over the dispatcher's window, had the names of fifteen or twenty ships chalked on it, with a list opposite each name of the jobs that were open on the ship. The one at the top was *Natoco Centaur*. It needed a bosun. He would throw in for that one when the next call started.

It was not easy to get a ship crewed any more. The jobs outnumbered the men. It had been that way for over two years now. In the old days, it was the other way around. Now, though, 1943, what with the war, shipping was wide open. Anybody could get out on a ship now. Kids, bums, winoes, anybody. Still, most of the people that went out were pretty much average-looking. People working for a living. Bums might go out once, but they wouldn't try it a second time.

Most of the men in the hall were in their middle and late twenties, early thirties. Nearly all the younger ones were thin, and some of them had a kind of stare in their eyes. It was a look that made them seem patient, as if something had hit them and they might sometime, or might not, figure out how bad. He had heard it called the thousand-yard stare.

Kiwi knew some of the people in the hall. One of them, Frank Tobin, he knew well. Tobin would probably spot him in a minute. Maybe Tobin had not signed on any ship yet. If Tobin was ready to go out again they could sign on the same one now. *Centaur.* He had been on that ship a few times before.

Tobin had seen him now. Tobin was coming over.

"You're sure an ugly son of a bitch," Tobin said.

The loudspeaker squealed. Then it was turned down.

"Uglier every time I see you. What brings you down here?"

"Looking for a job, I guess."

"Try the draft board, Luks. They got the kind of work for you. I'm glad to see you here, though. I mean I'm glad to see you at all. You heard about that *Richmond,* I guess?"

It had been sunk. That was what Tobin was going to tell him. Or blown up. Or blew itself up, caught fire by itself. That had happened, with tankers.

"What happened to it?"

"Sub got it," Tobin said. "Down by West Palm Beach, couple of weeks ago."

Hughes had been on the *Richmond*. Tobin would tell him soon how Hughes had made out.

The loudspeaker gave some scraping sounds. Then, the dispatcher's voice. "Okay, people. Got a few jobs here. Want a few men. *Natoco Centaur*. One bosun."

They were already standing at the dispatch window. Kiwi handed his union book to the window man. The window man had his left arm in a sling, with a cast on the forearm.

He looked at Tobin. "You want to g-go on this thing? They need some AB's, what the board says."

"You sure *you* want to go? You've got the stutters, sounds like to me. You've got a stare, too. Listen, Luks. You better not go out for a while yet. What do you think?"

"You want to go or don't you?"

"Not me, man. I know enough to stay off these fire traps.—I signed on already, Luks. Day before yesterday."

The loudspeaker. "All right, people. Two AB's. You're out there, I got to have you. A for Able, B for Bodied."

The window man gave him back his union book. And a pass card, stamped and signed. The card was to show the guard at the ship. It was stamped *Valid Until 4 PM 22 March 1943*. That was today. A four p.m. deadline probably meant the ship was leaving tonight.

The loudspeaker was going again. Still for AB's.

"Where you headed now, Luks?" Tobin said. "Let's go over here to Power's, okay?"

"I just left there."

"You can get back in, can't you? He didn't throw you out, did he?"

He needed to go over there again anyway. He had left his seabag there. Power's was a bar, across the street from the hall, and it had a free checkroom in the rear that people from the hall could use.

"I wish things had worked out for old Hughes, though," Tobin said. "He was a fine man. He was a fine man."

Hughes had made an issue of it, for him to get off the *Richmond*.
"Get your stuff packed up, Luks, okay?" That was the night they got
the ship docked, after it was tied up and the work had eased up. "I'll
help you get it together. You better bug off this thing for a while.
You're not decent company for us Social Register types." Until
eventually, he had agreed. But Hughes had stayed on.

"You say Simmons was the one telling you about it?"

"It was him," Tobin said. "Last week, was when I saw him. In
here, as a matter of fact."

"He know who else got out of it?"

"Not every one he didn't. The raft Simmons was in, it was only
Lopez and Grant and Hughes in it with him. So they were the only
ones he knew about for certain. He said it was two more rafts,
though, besides his. I guess you knew a good many on that
Richmond?"

"Lopez. I knew him to talk to."

"How about Hughes? I thought you and him were old timers."

He didn't say anything.

"Oh. Well, Grant and Lopez both got burned pretty bad. And
Lopez, he got his leg broke besides. Simmons just got his hands
burned. He had the bandages off one already. When I saw him in
here last week. Couldn't tell anything much had happened to it. And
them oil burns, they're bad ones. I guess you found that out,
though."

Tobin had been in the ship at Trinidad. His feet and ankles began
itching.

"You were lucky you got off that *Richmond*, Luks. You know
that?"

"Yes. Yes, I do."

"You know that George Washington Hotel in West Palm Beach?"

Tobin. Something about a hotel.

"Luks? In West Palm down there?"

"What about it?"

"Well, it's got this light on top of it. Simmons had been watching
it, see. They were along near West Palm, and there's this neon light
up on top of the hotel. All them places down there have lights. It

makes the ships stand out and the submarines can see one ten miles away, and still you can't get them people to turn their lights off. They say it would be bad for business. And Simmons saw the torpedo coming. Saw its track, you know. It's sort of pretty, except it's going to give you the finger. But what he was telling me, all that beach is patrolled down there. The Coast Guard drives up and down in jeeps, and Simmons said they have trained dogs in the jeeps. Mean dogs. They're trained to jump anybody except the particular Coast Guard people they're assigned to. And when Simmons and Lopez and Grant and Hughes, when they got out of the raft and got up on the beach, it was a couple of jeeps already there. *Richmond* sitting out there burning, and a whole crowd of people come out to watch, come out to see the show for Christ sake. And the dogs are mean already, and these here, they were excited on top of that about the fire. And all that crowd milling around. They were chained to the jeeps, but they were jumping and yelling, and the Coast Guard was blowing whistles? Yelling at the dogs?"

"Dogs jump Simmons?"

"They did. Jumped all four of them. It was two dogs, and they snapped the chains. Simmons and Grant, they were holding Lopez up between them since Lopez had his leg broke besides being burned. And Hughes right behind them, see. And these dogs come tearing over in a pair."

"I'd as soon contend with the fire myself. Jump back in the water."

"Not a lot of choice, is it? Except Hughes—Simmons and Grant had Lopez to take care of, you understand. But Hughes was right behind them, and it happened he had his shoes on still. About all he did have on, and half his hide burned off him besides. Some of it anyway. What he did, he got around in front of the other three. And he started in kicking one of the dogs, trying to, and he did manage to give it a couple of kicks in the head even the way it was jumping and dodging. Had some weight behind it too. Hughes damn near as big as you are. He got this one dog in the head, and it wasn't jumping so lively anymore. So then he got it again. And that time, he took care of it. It was just kind of crawling, then, and when it tried to stand up

it would fall over. But you know it was still trying for him? Just drag-
ging itself along, and it was still trying to get where it could get its
teeth in him. Simmons said if things had just been different, he'd
have liked for that dog to belong to him. But then, it was the other
one that was making the trouble. And it was going after Hughes. So
Simmons and Grant, they were trying to give Hughes a hand about
it. They just put Lopez down on the sand, and pitched in with
Hughes. It must have been a wild time, you know it? Rolling around
in the sand, fighting with a dog. And then they were killing it.
Because they'd realized from the way Hughes had done that they
could deal with it. Or anyway do all they could to. Since Hughes is
one of these people that don't go to pieces when something has to be
done. The Coast Guard boys got hold of their dog some way.
Rescued it. Chained it up again. You want some more liquor,
Luks?"

"I can choke it down."

"Can you now. Long as it pours, I think you can. Drink up."

Tobin nodded to the bartender, and the bartender brought two
more.

"But here's the way it ended up," Tobin said. "That first dog, that
one went ahead and died. It passed on. But it was a Coast Guard
dog, see, and so now, the Coast Guard? The government? What
they're doing, they're making them boys pay the price of that dog."

"Which boys?"

"Simmons and them. Grant, Lopez. They're to divide the cost of
it."

"Simmons not going to do it, is he?"

"He will not. Two hundred and forty-eight dollars. He showed me
the letter he got. Each one of the three of them, they got notification
from the government to make reimbursement. They're to divide it
three ways."

"I bet they won't do it. Three ways or any."

"Simmons told them nothing doing. And the Coast Guard said if
he don't, they'll have to attach it out of his pay. For destroying
government property."

"Hell they will. He better get the union to work on it."

"He's going to. That's what he was here in New York for, that day he was telling me about it. It would be divided four ways, see, except Hughes—well, he died that night in the hospital. He was burned pretty bad. And it was complications following burns . . . Simmons says he won't do it. He was in here last week, we had a couple drinks. He's staying over in Pennsylvania somewhere, he has relatives there. Let his hands finish healing up . . . Luks, where was it Hughes was from?"

"New York. Cortland. Upstate here."

"He have a family?"

"Wife. And a boy and a girl."

"He was a fine man. All the time, just as clean? Just as steady?"

The town was how he had first got acquainted with Hughes. He himself had lived in Ithaca, and Ithaca was near Cortland, and that made a sort of connection. Hughes, David Owen. Able Seaman. Age 31.

Now, Hughes was out of it. Hughes had beat the game. No more hopping for him, and he was in the clear now.

The bar was getting crowded. Quarter till twelve. The eleven-thirty call was over.

"You ready to shove off?" Tobin said. "Come have some chow, okay? I'll call the wife and tell her. She kept the kids in from school today, too."

Tobin only lived a few blocks away. He had two boys in grade school. But Tobin and his family ought to have the time to themselves. That was why she had kept the kids in.

"I can't make it, Frank. Thanks a lot anyway."

"You sure? You know you're welcome."

"I know, sure. Thanks anyway, man."

He needed to go to the bank, and turn in the Amex checks. He would call Denise first, and she could meet him at the bank. There was one across the street from the hotel. He would make them out to her. Or anyway arrange for her to have them. He was not going to be needing them.

"There's something I wish you'd do for me, though, Frank. If it won't load you up too much."

"Sure, man. What is it?"

He would also get his insurance changed, so it could go to her.

"This seabag I got here. You take it out to the ship for me? It's in the backroom. I'll give you the checktag for it."

"Sure. I'll do that. The wife's going to be driving me to the ship. I'll just put it in with my own debris."

Tobin had something he was not ever going to have. Hughes did too. A family. He was not going to get back. He had told her he was, but he realized now it was not going to happen. He had been Spoken to, and it was, now, very nearly over. And all of it had gone by so fast.

When he got up, he had to stand still for a minute. His feet had gone to sleep again. It happened now and then, since the burns. Tobin put a hand on his arm, but he could walk okay by then.

Tobin had paid for the drinks, so he left the baksheesh for the bartender. A dollar bill. The bartender was telling them Come in again, fellows.

He found the check for the seabag, and gave it to Tobin. He told Tobin he wanted to go back uptown for a while, and Tobin told him You bet, man.

Outside, they shook hands.

"See you later on, Luks."

"Right. See you."

Tobin went on.

He would get a ring for her. He had till four o'clock before he needed to be at the ship. That would give them time to pick one out. Two rings. One for each of them.

They would get lunch somewhere. She knew several places that had theater and show business customers. Theater girls were pretty. All of them together, though, could not be a match for her. He would not have made it, except for her. It was only on account of her that he had been able to keep his head above water. He thought that in some way she knew it too. He was sure of it. She could not have been dreaming he was watching her, without knowing that. More than that. When the time came, she had stood by him. There had only been three weeks, but how many people could say they had had that much. He was the luckiest soul alive.

He waited at the curb. A taxi would be by soon. Cabs took this street a lot when they were in the neighborhood, for the business from the hall.

During breakfast one morning, something that felt like rumbling, not quite loud enough to be heard, stirred in the ship, and faded out. In a few seconds, it came again. Wylie Dorrance was on his feet by that time, and at the exit from the galley. Dorrance and Arnold Chancellor were in the same cabin, and Arnold had noticed that Dorrance was always fast at getting out of the cabin, or any place, whenever a new sound happened. Wylie Dorrance had spoken of it himself once. He was ashamed of it. "Chancellor, I must be the most chicken bastard anywhere." Wylie was still at the galley exit now, not going any farther but not able to come on back.

Kiwi Luks came in, and said there had been a submarine alarm. The rumblings were from depth charges. The convoy's corvettes were throwing the charges, to keep a sort of fence of explosions around the ship.

Kiwi was speaking to Dorrance. "You got an appointment somewhere, Wylie?"

Dorrance came back to his place at the table. He still looked ready to leave again fast.

The first time, the rumbling made ripples in the bowl of beef soup Chancellor had in front of him. It did the other times also, and in his coffee. Caskie the steward gave them soup for breakfast, if they wanted any. Most of them did. With hot soup, people coming off topside could get warm quick, and people going on topside could stay warm a little longer. After a few times, Chancellor wished he had not noticed the ripples. He had become aware that they were happening inside him as well as in the bowls and cups. It would be easy to get sick again.

The other people, even Kiwi Luks, were probably also having ripples. Nobody wanted fried eggs. When the messman asked them how they wanted their eggs, they said hardboiled.

It came to Chancellor that the ripples were from nerves, instead of from the vibrations the charges made. From fear. The same thing that had Wylie Dorrance ready to be out the door again. Wylie was the only one that had jumped up, but it was the same thing.

The men coming off watch from topside, however, were doing well enough. One man, Larry Stack, one of a pair of twins, came stomping in pounding his doubled right hand into the palm of the other one. "Where's that Goddamn steward-looking Hugh Caskie? Tell him Larry Stack is here. Tell him Walter Stack is here too, and we're going to eat him out of house and home." Larry Stack sat down next to Chancellor. "Cold out there, people. Cold enough to freeze your balls off. And when they land on the deck, they go clink clink. Don't they, Walter?" Larry Stack was noisy. His brother Walter never had much to say. "That's the little ones. Big ones like me and Walter's, they go bonk bonk."

Leonard Norris looked disapproving. He was one of the AB's. Arnold Chancellor had noticed that he looked disapproving about almost anything.

Larry Stack jabbed an elbow against Arnold. "How you doing, Youngun?" People called him Youngun sometimes, or Kid, or Junior. Stack spoke to the messman. "Go see if the steward has Youngun's formula warmed, will you?"

Arnold himself, when he was outside, felt okay again. There was no wind to speak of, but the air was extremely cold. They were in the high sixties latitudes, now, north of Iceland, polar latitudes. He was wearing a hood and a heavy fleece-lined jacket and gloves and two pairs of trousers, and hightop fleece-lined shoes, but the cold still got in.

Kiwi Luks had assigned him, with Wylie Dorrance and a man named Everett Lessing, and Leonard Norris, to inspect lifeboats. They needed to check the launching gear for the boats, the davits and cables and brakes and pulleys that would swing the boats out from the ship and let them down if the time came. They were also checking the supplies and equipment in the boats. Norris was in charge of the job. Wylie Dorrance knew the inspection procedure, and Everett Lessing also did, but Norris pointed out each item anyway, and told them what it was for, and had one of the three of them read off the checklist to the other two, item by item. Wylie Dorrance had said that Norris, even though he was an AB, had probably not been in charge of many jobs. Did not know how to be in charge.

"The reason this is so important, men," Norris said, "people's lives can depend on what we're doing."

"You wouldn't kid me, would you?" Dorrance said. Dorrance had once had to abandon ship. The cable and pulley that were holding the front end of the boat he was in, gave way. The boat was hanging by its other end. Dorrance and all the others in the boat, some of them already injured, fell the rest of the way.

The boats needed to have water and food and blankets, maps and medicine. Lifeboats had sometimes not had all their supplies. People had stolen them. The medicine included a morphine compound, in syrettes, for pain-killer. Whenever anything was stolen it was likely to be the syrettes. In ports, people could get high prices for them. Dorrance said he had made a trip once with a man who had kept the rest of the crew from beating up a fellow that had been caught with a supply of stolen syrettes. "You know the man I'm talking about, Chancellor. The one that kept the guy from getting beat up. Take a guess who it was."

Arnold thought. "Luks?"

"Sure it was. Kiwi Luks. He's a lot of man, you know it? Year before last was when it was. We were in Port Arthur, Texas."

In the open, here on deck, the rumblings did not come through as strong as they had during breakfast. Maybe it was necessary to be inside the ship for them to be felt.

The people down in the engine room were probably feeling them strong. The engine room was far down. Getting out of it would take a long time.

The first time Arnold had seen Kiwi, back in New York, he had seen that Kiwi was a man of authority. Dorrance had told him later that Kiwi was the bosun. At the time, he was, but after the trip started he was a sort of Third Mate. The ship had not got a full crew, and the Captain, Swicker, had told him to take over as Third. People did not have to call him Mister, though. Swicker did, so as to back him up, but Luks had told the people in the crew not to. Arnold had seen also, or at least had the impression, that Luks had somewhere along been under great stress, more than Luks himself was going to let himself know about for a time yet. But there was something else besides in Kiwi's face. A message, of some kind. Arnold did not know what it was, but he was certain he had seen it there.

The convoy was a big one now. At Reykjavik, back at Iceland, several small ones had joined up. Fifty-three ships in all, and there was also the escort. In addition to corvettes and DE's, the escort included a cruiser, and a carrier. They were going to Murmansk, in Russia. Long cold trip. People said it was the most dangerous one of all.

Word had circulated about where they were going before they reached Iceland. People had told Stack he might see some of his cousins. The Stacks were Canadian, from Vancouver, and their grandparents were Russian, by way of Alaska. Before their father changed it, their last name had been Stalcevsky.

One man, Stanley Barton, had cracked up when it became known that they were going to be on the Murmansk Run. Back then, people had not had any way of being sure about it, but Barton had still gone to pieces. They knew now, because of the size of the convoy and because it had not only a cruiser but an aircraft carrier, that they were in fact headed either for Murmansk, or Archangel. The ships had also been going north since they had left Iceland. If they had only been going to England, they would almost be there by now. They would not have had such heavy protection either. The carrier was what was going to count. It was not a big one, but it was still a carrier. It had airplanes, English Hurricanes, fighter planes, and that was what mattered.

Luks. In Port Arthur, he had kept the man from getting beat up. When Stanley Barton cracked up, some of the people here on the *Centaur* had called him yellow, and Luks had told them not so. Luks knew him from previous trips, and he said that on those, Barton had done his share, and more. But Barton had got too close to the edge, been pushed too close, had finally gone over. People had been surprised. He had looked to be in good shape. He had been working all right, acting all right.

He had started saying then that people were talking about him. The talkers were in his home town, Providence, Rhode Island. He knew who they were, and some of what they were saying, and that they knew where he was. They were using acoustics to keep track of him. The ship's route and location needed to be kept secret, and now that the Providence people knew where he was, the crew was in danger.

Barton disappeared. It was possible he had jumped overboard, and Kiwi had people begin searching the ship for him. It was Arnold who had found him, in one of the lifeboats. Barton was under some blankets, six of them, with his knees pulled up to his chin. Arnold spoke to him, and Barton said Hello there, Junior. Kiwi came up, and Barton explained that being in the lifeboat, and using the blankets, gave some insulation against the acoustics. Kiwi decided to let him stay there. The Captain, Swicker, said that Barton would have to go ashore when the ship reached Iceland. The Navy had a hospital there. Later on, Barton could be returned to Boston or New York.

Barton had not wanted to leave his lifeboat. It meant safety to him, and the blankets meant six wrappings of safety. Kiwi himself took him food, during the day and a half Barton was in it.

Inspecting lifeboats. At nine-thirty, Frank Tobin came along, to see how the work was going. Tobin had become bosun, when Luks moved up. They had checked four boats by that time. Tobin said they were going too slow. "Norris, you got all four of you working on one boat at a time? That'll take all day. Pair off, work on two at a time."

Norris paused. "Any way you want it done, Tobin."

"Two guys at a time." Tobin moved on.

"We're going to change things around a little," Norris said. His voice was sharp. "Which two will it—wait a minute. Dorrance, you come with me. Lessing, you and this kid here."

Dorrance elbowed Everett Lessing. "That means you get him, don't it? I wanted him."

Lessing smiled. He was older than either of them. "But I got him."

Norris was muttering something.

"I think Norris is sort of cute too, though," Dorrance said.

"Chancellor is the cutest. Look at him blushing."

Norris was angry. "Chancellor, you and this guy move up to that next boat. Dorrance, we'll finish this one. All right, what are you standing around for?"

Arnold and Lessing went on to the next one. They had to make their way around blocks of crates to get to it. All the deck space was taken up with crates, strapped and cabled together and bolted to the deck.

Dorrance had only been fooling around back there, but Everett Lessing actually was queer. Most of the people in the ship, if they gave any attention to it, only kidded Lessing, and he kidded back. He worked well, and he had several years of seatime. He looked rugged. What he did for pastime, however, was sewing. Some of the people painted, or read, or just slept, in their spare time. One man, Tucker Vance, played a guitar and practiced with his guitar. Vance was from Arnold's part of the country, the mountains, and mostly he played mountain songs. Lessing, however, made shirts, and mended things. He had lengths of cloth, and a fitted leather case of needles and thread and buttons. He was expert at sewing and mending, and people were glad to have his work. Clothes got torn every day.

At ten-thirty, Tobin came around again, and told them they could get coffee and cake in the galley. Arnold and Lessing had finished five boats. Dorrance and Leonard Norris had finished three.

The depth-charging had stopped by then. Arnold had not noticed when it ended. No more ripples.

Wylie Dorrance put a greater quantity of sugar in his coffee. He had very bad teeth, probably from the amount of sugar and candy he ate. He had cartons and metal cans of taffy and mints and chocolate in his locker. He had said he had started once to get some repairs on his teeth, but while he was waiting in the dentist's office he had got to thinking about the picks and the drills, and after a few minutes of thinking about them he made tracks. He had told Arnold and their other cabinmate, George Rand, to help themselves to the candy whenever they wanted any. Rand kept forgetting where it stayed. Year before last, a ship that Rand and Kiwi were on was at London, and it got bombed. Rand had been hit in the head, and his memory was damaged. A good part of it had come back, for things that had happened some time in the past, but he had trouble keeping track of things that had happened a few weeks ago, or a day or two ago. It got him embarrassed to keep asking where the candy was. When Wylie Dorrance realized it did, he began leaving some of it out on the table in the cabin. Rand had kept forgetting where the convoy was going. Eventually he wrote it down on a piece of paper, "Murmansk Run," and put the paper in his wallet.

They got the lifeboat-checking finished at one-thirty. Long watches, on this ship. This one had been nearly six hours. Four hours was regular length, but the crew was short, and people worked extra time. Now, though, they could go off duty for a while.

Fog was coming in again. Fog was a break, as long as it did not get really thick. In a fog, or rough weather, the ships would be hard for a submarine to see, to aim for. There was fog now several times a day, but no high wind anymore. Summertime. The month of July. Long days. Even at midnight the sun was still visible, low towards the horizon.

Arnold was getting ready to follow Dorrance down the ladder, back to their cabin. Behind him then, somebody was saying something. It was Lessing, and it sounded like Lessing had said something about a submarine. That was in fact what he had said. "Good Christ Goddamn. There's a sub over there."

Lessing, sharp-sighted, had seen the periscope. There was the torpedo track then, the line of bubbles lengthening towards the carrier. The submarine had been inside the convoy. All morning. All this time. The sound of the ships' engines had kept it from being picked up on the sonar.

The torpedo track was reaching the carrier. A plane was letting down onto the carrier deck. The plane's nose was high, and it had touched then, accepted the deck surface. Sirens and yelpers were going off on the ships. Anyhow on the ones in the distance. They sounded like young birds peeping for the parent birds. Back at home, a pair of robins had built a nest year after year in a rhododendron bush that grew by the front porch of Arnold's house. One year, in May, a storm blew the nest out of the tree one night, and the young robins were dead on the ground the next morning. The yelpers on the nearby ships began. On this one too they did. Then, though, he realized they had already been going. It was only the surprise that had made him think they were distant. Here and there, a few ships were blurry, through the fog patches. The plane that had touched down, and all the other planes on the carrier, bounced around. People were being thrown, scattered around, on the carrier deck. The carrier had exploded then. One burst, yellow and blue-white and red.

He had had some thought that the trip might go well after all. Most of them had had some such idea. It was, he knew now, running now to get to his Fire Control Point, looking for Rand in case Rand did not remember, out of the question. The tanker had not been hit, but people were getting to the Points they had been assigned to anyway. Sonar had not helped, nothing else had. Nothing was going to, enough to count. All that was in the question now, all that had been the whole time, was how bad they were not going to make it. What was going to be left, by the time it was over.

The weather became rough again. Days without wind, rough water, became the unusual ones. They were moving into a high-pressure zone. Kiwi knew it by the wind-rule. One of the first trips he had ever made, an old old man had told him about it. Wind travelled clockwise around a high-pressure zone, if it was north of the equator. When anybody stood with his back to the wind, in northern latitudes, the high-pressue region would be to the right. That old man had said they could check it by the glass. He meant by the barometer, and he was right. Later, Luks found that the wind direction, and the pressure-zone location, were involved with the Coriolis phenomenon. Maybe the spiral nebulae also were. He kept thinking lately about the cycles of things. The turnings, and the turnings. The ocean, the air, were only films, compared to the earth itself. Maybe the spiral nebulae and all the universe were only a film on something else.

Why Coriolis. Maybe somebody's name. An Italian maybe by the name of Coriolis. There was somebody on the ship who would know. Not Tobin. Not George Rand either, although Rand knew some astronomy. He could not think of the person's name.

The wind now was from the south. That meant that the high-pressure zone was to the east. Ahead of them. The convoy was moving almost due east. The course had been north at first, from Iceland, but all that was over with now. Norway, the North Cape, was a few hundred miles ahead, and to the south. They would keep it as far to the south as possible, in order to get the most distance from the planes that would be coming from Norway, the German bomber bases, to knock off any ships that might try to get to Murmansk.

The first Murmansk and Archangel convoys, back in 1941 and early 1942, had been mainly for politics. They had been efforts at persuading the Russians to keep fighting. Eventually there had been more ships, and more machinery and guns and food for them to carry, and the convoys were having some military effect. Last year, there had been an extra big one. Something went wrong, though. The escort that had started with it was called off, and the convoy was smashed. Kiwi had met some survivors from that one. It was called the Fourth of July Convoy, and he had heard it called PQ 17. A code designation. They said there had been a plan to use it for bait. The Germans had two battleships, and the idea was that if the escort left, the battleships would come out to attack the convoy and they could be sunk. It was a smart idea, and it worked out about as well as most smart ideas. The Germans didn't want to play battleship, and nearly every one of the ships in the Fourth of July Convoy and the men on them were eliminated. The survivors were bitter. Seamen in general were, after the word got around. None of the smart-idea people had bothered to find out if they wanted to be bait.

It was possible that this convoy now was going to be bait. The types who made such plans as the one for PQ-17 were slow learners, and what had happened might not have made any impression on them. Still, if they let two convoys get ruined, they might not be

planners any longer. That was probably the reason for the heavy
escort this one had. Used to have. The carrier was gone now. And it
was the carrier, the airplanes, that would have made the difference.

He would write to Denise again. He had been writing to her every
day, and he would start adding to the accumulation again. At Iceland he had sent eighteen letters to her. A bundle of letters from her
had been waiting for him.

The wind increased. The ships had reached the edge of a storm,
and topside work was called off. There was rain, horizontal in the
wind. Getting from the wheelhouse to crew quarters involved being
outside, and it was labor.

Arnold had wheel watch once. The rain streamed and streamed
against the glass of the wheelhouse. It was hard to see what was out
there. He himself did not actually need to. He only needed to keep to
the compass heading the Mate gave him. Wedeck, the First Mate,
was on duty, and that was a break. When Wedeck or Kiwi gave instructions, all they did was give instructions. The other Mate, Courtney, made it sound as if he would do people a favor and let them
obey him. Courtney didn't like it that Kiwi was an Acting Mate, and
whenever he said Mister Luks, he emphasized the Mister.

The wind got stronger still. The rain became sleet, and Captain
Swicker, and then Kiwi, were in and out of the wheelhouse. Swicker
and Kiwi and Wedeck took turns at going out onto the bridge, where
there was no protection. They wore hoods, and facemasks, and goggles, and whenever one of them came back inside, his hood was iced
over, and bearded with ice.

This was not a real storm. In a real one, Larry Stack said, he
would have been hanging over the wheel-spokes to keep from falling
down. Norris said there would have been someone else for wheelman
in the first place, a person with experience, if the weather had
amounted to anything.

By the time Arnold's next watch came around, the rain and sleet
had stopped, and the wind had let up. People could work outside
again. Some of the crates of deck cargo had come loose, and they
needed to be secured to the deck again. Two of them had broken

open. They had refrigerators, home-size electric iceboxes. "Taking Goddamn iceboxes to Murmansk," Dorrance said. "I knew I ought to got some other trip besides this one."

Dorrance stopped working, and listened. He went back to work. "Thought I might hear them planes." He meant the ones from Norway.

The wind picked up again. This time it was from the north. It brought floating ice, and the ships were moving through chunks and floes of it.

The ice got thicker. Pack ice, almost, and the ships had to change course. The convoy was slanting southeast then. Towards land.

The next morning, two planes that looked like bombers came in sight. They were patrol planes. "Looks like they found us," Stack said.

But more fog came in. Thick fog. Maybe it would last. Maybe there would be fog all the rest of the way. It kept them from seeing any of the other ships, but it kept the airplanes from seeing them. The convoy slowed down. Collisions could happen in the fog. Being in the fog was still safe, though, compared to being in the open, where the planes could spot them.

Horns. Hoarse, baying, unceasing. It came to Arnold that the sound they made was the ultimate sound for being on a ship. It was close to being the reason for being on one. People called him Junior sometimes. They called him Kid. They considered him a kid, somebody not to be taken seriously. They felt that the only reason he was able to be in the crew, and he realized they were right, was the shortage of people. They could call him anything. Anything they called him and considered him would be worth it, for having heard the horns in the polar fog.

There was no way of knowing when it was night, when day. Clocks gave the hours, but in the fog there was neither light nor darkness. People lost their sense of balance, direction, time, when they were topside. Sometimes the relief watch was coming on before people had been ten minutes on their own watch. So it seemed, or the next one never got there, and they waited. And waited.

The fog left. It disappeared one afternoon, in a matter of minutes.

Sun, brilliant. Clouds, but they were cirrus clouds, thin and high. A breeze. This was the kind of weather a high-pressure system was supposed to have. The ice was gone. All during the fog, there had been ice. The ship had kept bumping pieces of it. Each time, there had been, for part of a second, during sleep or what counted for sleep, during any time but especially during sleep, the possibility that it was a mine the ship had hit. Getting over the possibility took a long time. Respiration, pulse rate, belly muscles, speeded up and tightened up, and they took a long time to get back to their regular rates and get related to each other again.

Far out, from the south, up towards the cirrus, a row of small planes appeared. Four. Another row, higher, came in sight, and behind that one, higher again, still another. Fast, high, thin-sounding. They had been expected for several days now. Now they were here.

On the cruiser, the convoy's command ship, a new set of signal flags were going up. Blinker lights were busy from the cruiser to the other ships. The convoy began spreading out. Lengthening out. So as to be a harder target. Collection of targets.

On the *Centaur*, the Navy gun crews were already at their locations. The ship's crew were hurrying to their own. There was no confusion. Lessing and Wylie Dorrance, Arnold and George Rand, were assigned to the same gun, the one on top of the wheelhouse. Rand remembered his location, this time.

None of the guns on the ships were going yet. The planes were still a long way out. Still high.

The planes were turning, then, dropping. Turning again, much lower now, sliding in. Lessing said they were torpedo planes. ME-110's.

The DE's had started firing. Some of the cargo ships, the ones the planes would reach first, had started.

It was confusing how fast the planes were, now that they were close in. Out in the distance they looked sort of slow. They were pointed to the cruiser, instead of to the cargo ships. The cruiser had anti-aircraft guns, many of them, and they were firing. Some of the big ones were firing into the water instead of directly towards the planes, into the track the planes would be taking, and fountains were bursting out of the water. The planes would need to fly into them. Or else change course.

Torpedoes were dropping away from the planes. The planes that had deposited their torpedoes were sliding upwards, over the cruiser. Outwards away from it. Each one had separate cones of tracers following it.

One plane, that had not finished its run, blew up. It paused, and part of it disappeared, and smoke, yellow fire, swelled out from where it had been.

A plane crashed into the water. The cruiser was changing course. The planes wanted it at right angles to them, so as to have the length of it for a target. This way they would be reaching it at a sharper angle. Before it finished the course change, the planes were gone. All of them that were left, ten, were out beyond it already, climbing again. The attack was over.

It had not lasted a full five minutes. The cruiser had not been hit. None of the torpedoes had got to it. And instead, two of the planes had been knocked down.

Lessing, Rand, Dorrance, were opening and closing their hands. Arnold found he was doing the same thing. He probably had been, his hands had, all this time. Inside his gloves, his hands were sweaty.

He began being aware of the sounds that had been taking place. The airplanes. The closer they got, the worse they had sounded. Under that one, gunfire. From the distance it had sounded like popcorn. And under that one, something rolling. The big guns on the cruiser.

In the galley he was still hearing them. The planes were gone, for the time being, and some of the people off duty had gone to the galley, but the sounds, some of them, kept on anyway. Seemed to. The convoy had been attacked. Anyway the cruiser had been. Yet, what about it? It should have amounted to more than it had.

People were saying in the galley that it was foolish for torpedo planes to go against a big ship. That had been tried many times, and it had never worked out. Somebody else said not to talk too soon. The convoy had only just come in range of airplanes. It only had a few ships that were armored. There were many more planes. Bigger ones. There had never been a ship, armored or any kind, that could stand up to planes.

Next morning, more appeared. They did not come in close. Three, big ones. Patrol bombers. Focke-Wulfes, Condors. They circled the convoy, not very fast, big and black, out of gun range. The DE's tried to rush into range, but the Condors each time climbed, just enough to be too far out for them.

All that day they followed the ships. At night also, although it never got to be night in the way anybody was used to. This was too far north for any actual dark, this time of year.

The Condors were stalking them. If only the carrier had not been sunk. Eighteen planes. That was how many it had had, and all of them, every one, were gone. The ones that had not been on the carrier at the time, their pilots had finally pointed them away from the convoy, and jumped. Parachuted, and one of the DE's had picked them out of the water.

The morning after that, the Condors were still there. Not hardly the same ones. Three of them, even so, that looked the same, sounded the same, as the first ones.

He could not remember when he had seen a sky so blue. When the sea had been so clear. Tucker Vance played music for them. The fantail had some clear space, and they gathered there, and Vance picked his guitar. End of July now. Maybe it was August already. They had been out from home so long, and whenever Arnold missed a day at checking the calendar, whenever any of them did, they lost command of knowing which day it was.

If the weather stayed warm, they could move north again. It did stay warm, but the ice increased again. This quantity of it, this time of the year, was freakish. They could not go farther north after all.

The day after that, four p.m., more bombers arrived. Arnold heard them long before they came in sight. By the sound, they were numerous. Yet when they got close enough to be seen—Kiwi found them first, with binoculars—they were not so many. Only six. That was enough. That was all there would need to be.

He was already at his location, with the gun, by the time they were visible. Lessing and the others were. They had known, everybody had, because of the Condors, because they themselves and their ships were out here, in the open, that more planes would be here.

But even this time, nothing much happened. These planes now stayed high. The guns could not reach them, but they were too high for their bombs to hit anything either. It was hard to tell if the planes had any particular ship in mind. All the bombs, four from each plane, struck the water, and went off, and when the water had subsided, that was all there was. The planes had already turned south again.

But by that time, more were arriving. They came in from the north instead of from the south. They looked like the ME-110's, the torpedo planes. However, they were not carrying torpedoes this time. They were still trying for the cruiser, and they turned out to be dive bombers. They showed up so suddenly, and they dropped so fast, that it was hard to make out what they were doing, until they were in process of doing it. Guns from every ship around and from the cruiser itself were firing at them, the empty cartridges from this gun, Lessing and Rand working the gun, Arnold and Dorrance there for standby, rattling on the roof. The guns were having trouble tracking the planes. The planes were moving too fast, dropping too fast, and explosions were happening on the cruiser. It had been hit. The dive bombers had got it. Explosions. And then, masses of smoke. Two different kinds. All of it was dark, but some of it, instead of rising, settled towards the water.

He did not see Wylie Dorrance. Dorrance had cut out for somewhere. Only himself and Lessing and George Rand were at the gun. Lessing and Rand had stopped firing. The dive bombers were gone. The cruiser was giving off huge quantities of smoke. Greasy-looking. Heavy.

Gunpowder smell. It came from here. It came from all over. The air had become hazy, from all the gunfire. He had had a toy pig once, made out of celluloid. He and his brother had set fire to it one day, with matches his brother had swiped from the kitchen, and it had blazed up, and made a nitrate smell.

The dive bombers again. They had hit the cruiser again. And once again left. The cruiser had become only something that gave off black and yellowish smoke. Spurted out streamers of fire.

An interval without airplanes. It got longer.

The smoke was not so thick anymore. The fire spurts had stopped. The smoke was stopping.

He heard some hollering. It was the Armed Guard people. The Navy people, and they were cheering. The other Navy people, the men on the cruiser, had got the fires put out, got their ship in hand. It had taken and held up under two separate strikes by dive bombers, and the Navy men here on the tanker were cheering and hollering, shaking hands with each other. He found that he was yelling with them. Kiwi was shaking hands with somebody in the Armed Guard.

He had seen something in Kiwi's face once. More than once. A message. It was something like a message. That Kiwi had come to know, had been Told, that his time was getting towards being finished. Arnold had not known at the time what he had seen. He thought that now he did.

Still no more airplanes. It was possible that this would be all for the day.

That was in fact all, and the planes were not back the next day either. One of the Condors left. Two stayed, keeping watch. The ships had to go still farther south. The ice was moving south, and the ships had to stay in reasonably ice-clear water. The ice was pushing them into easier reach of the airplanes.

Dorrance had a hard time facing people anymore. He had run, when the cruiser was getting worked over. It was not this ship at all, it was the cruiser, and still he had run. Had left Rand, Chancellor, Lessing, to work the gun by themselves. Chancellor was a rookie, Lessing was some kind of queer, Rand didn't have all his brain working anymore. But he was the one that had run.

He had left so fast because he had shit his pants. He wanted to get away before the others noticed. Afterwards he realized he must have shit himself so as to have a reason for leaving. He realized then that the others would have been too busy, were too busy, had other matters on their mind, to notice. As a reason, it had not been worth much. Dive bombers howling, the cruiser fighting back hard, most of the other ships firing, bombs exploding, and that was the time he had picked to let his sphincter come loose.

This was the way things were going to be with him, then. He would not have any clean pants left before long. The ones he had fouled, he had thrown overboard.

He had thought that someway or other things would turn out better. He knew he was yellow, but he had thought that when the time came he would be able to stand up to it.

Now he knew better. Now he did.

Two days after the first dive bombers were there, more arrived. The Condors must have sent word that the cruiser was still operating. The alarm came at four in the morning. Full daylight already. Now that it was clear weather, planes could see the ships easy all the time. Arnold counted eighteen planes. Six V's, with three in each V. They concentrated on the cruiser.

He had to leave off with counting and watching, because after they had started, more arrived. The others were torpedo planes. He had an impression that they were not aiming the torpedoes. They were sowing them, into the convoy. Sometimes the torpedoes kept bouncing in and out of the water. Porpoising. Sometimes they swerved left and right. It did not matter much what they did. They were likely to hit some ship regardless. He had heard of torpedoes that were designed to swerve. Maybe the ones now were that kind.

One of the ammo ships got hit. Something spurted upwards out of it, fire, extremely fast, high. A wad of fire, a globe of it, red and yellow, and then all the ship had exploded. It was not close by, but the heat flash still stung his face. He noticed by the stinging that he had forgotten to put his face mask on. He had been sleeping in his clothes. All of them had been. They had fire-resistant clothing, including hoods and masks, but he had forgotten his. The ammo ship explosion kept climbing. There must have been a sound. He thought that he had in fact heard a roar. It was hard to be sure exactly what he had heard, in the general uproar. Ships were dodging the torpe-does. Trying to dodge them. He saw one that looked on course to run into another one. He didn't get a chance to see how it worked out. The fire from the ammo ship had stopped rising. Smoke was spreading from the top of it. An umbrella. He was sure he had heard the roar. A waterfall. A train in a tunnel. Lessing was handling the gun. Lessing was only firing when a plane looked close enough to be hit. That was not many times. Some of them had been hit anyway, and all around and among the ships the water was exploding from where the planes had struck.

Maybe things were calming down. The torpedo planes were gone. The others were, the dive bombers. The noise was over with.

The cruiser was leaning bad. The middle of it was torn up. Smoke was drifting out of it. The sailors were leaving it. Some of them were in boats, some were climbing down a net and getting into boats that were waiting for them. Two of the DE's had come near, and the boats were en route to the DE's.

His ears were ringing. Things did not look right. There was trouble making out how they were supposed to look. The other people, from the way their faces were, he saw there must be something of the same thing with them. Things did not look right to them either. Yet he could not tell what was wrong with the way they looked.

People on the deck of the cruiser, the few who were still on it, were crawling now. The cruiser was leaning too much, the deck was too slanted, for them to be able to stand. They were getting to the net, climbing along it.

Somebody was speaking to him. Tobin. How you doing, kid. He was answering Tobin. Okay, I guess. Tobin was telling them that as soon as they got the empty cartridges cleaned away they ought to check in at the galley. Right away there would be some breakfast.

Five-thirty. An hour and a half. The planes had got here at four.

In the afternoon, more of them. Two-engine bombers. They were slow compared to the others, but that was no drawback to them, now. The cruiser had sunk, many miles back, and without the cruiser, the planes did not have much to bother about. Bombers, and also single-engine planes. Everybody wanted to get on it.

Arnold was on wheel watch when they showed up. It was nearly time for changing watches. Courtney, the Second Mate, came in and took the wheel and told him to go bring some coffee. What with the bombs and the gunfire he was not about to be running around bringing coffee. Before he had time to say anything, Courtney was speaking again.

"What are you waiting for, boy?—Wait, wait, hold it. Hold it, hold it."

Swicker had been hit. Captain Swicker, outside, on the bridge. There was blood, and Swicker was on his knees. He was getting himself up again. Kiwi was out there, and Wedeck, and they were lifting him. He was standing by himself then. The deck out there had a line of holes in it. Bullet holes. They looked like holes from hammering spikes into the metal.

Swicker passed out. Arnold and Kiwi and somebody else, Larry Stack, got him to his cabin. The medic, Bailey, got there. When they got Swicker's jacket and sweater and shirt off him, one of the rib bones was sticking out through his heavy wool undershirt. The end sticking out was jagged. The undershirt had a patch of blood, that got bigger. Bailey gave him an injection, in the left arm. The mattress was getting bloody. Whatever had hit him had not got to his lungs. Larry Stack said there would be blood and froth coming out of his nose, if the lung had been hit. Stack had been in pre-med school before he began shipping. Bailey the medic was packing the bullet holes with gauze, to try and slow down the bleeding. They were tears, rips, more than holes. Stack was helping him. Swicker was talking, sort of, but he was not conscious, and he was not struggling. He stopped talking. Then it was all over. Both his legs kicked out, and then he had relaxed and his eyes had opened and the whites were showing.

Bailey had to get back to the sickbay. There was nothing more that could be done for Swicker, and the sickbay had people who needed attending to.

Kiwi told Arnold to go to his gun position, on top of the wheelhouse. "Fasten this on you first," Kiwi said. He drummed with his fingers on the flak helmet Arnold was wearing. Arnold began buckling the strap under his chin.

Luks was looking at him. "You ever hear of the Coriolis effect?"

"The Coriolis force? I've heard of that."

"You know what it is?"

"Something about the weather. Centrifugal force."

"Who's it named after? Do you know?"

"This Frenchman. Gaspard Coriolis."

"You sure?"

"Yessir. Pretty sure. How come you're asking me?"

"I just figured you'd be the one that would know. Get on up there now, okay?"

"Yessir."

Over to the south, planes were busy at a DE. Closer in, one of the merchant ships had been hit. It was sinking. Another plane headed for it. Single-engine plane. The forward guns on the hit ship were still above water, and still firing. Lessing and the other *Centaur* gunners concentrated on the plane. It passed at right angles, low. The pilot had goggles and a helmet and something over his mouth, a cup or mask. The plane's guns were firing, wing guns, at the ship that was already done for. The pilot's head snapped backwards against the headboard his seat had. Lessing, somebody, had got him. His plane crashed between the two ships. It was broken, but it was floating, and the guns that could be aimed towards it kept firing at it, until it was cut to pieces.

The other planes had left.

People were laughing, going over what had happened, squabbling about the details. After a time they were getting quiet. Before long, the letdown took them.

Kiwi and Tobin got them busy at cleaning up. They were sweeping away the empty cartridges, cleaning and re-loading the guns. Lessing and the others who had actually been handling the guns went off duty then. Arnold and the others stayed on, in case the planes came back, until the gunners could get something to eat.

Word went around that Swicker was dead. Two of the Armed
Guard people had been injured. Several men on the crew had been,
but not from gunfire. They had fallen, or got their fingers mashed,
or been cut. A number of new people were on board. They were from
the ship that had been sunk. Two other ships, and one of the DE's,
were gone.

People were shaving, washing up, changing clothes. They had
sweated a lot. Things were quiet now. Nobody was saying much. In
the galley, and in the cabins, they had the lights dimmed. There was
too much light outside, and people's eyes were irritated.

They were in the galley. It would be chowtime soon. Supper.
Arnold wanted to go to sleep. He had dropped off to sleep, twice, in
his cabin, but both times he had imagined he heard a pretty bad
sound somewhere. The noise of the ammo ship when it went up, and
to keep from hearing it he went ahead and stayed awake. Some of
the other people, nearly all of them, were drowsing off, and then
waking up fast.

Ten-thirty the next morning was when the next planes arrived.
People had been hearing them for some time. There was a breeze,
from the south, and it had carried the engine sound. The planes were
in two formations. Triangles, fifteen in each, two-engine bombers.

"Goddamn," Rand said "Them bastards really mean it, don't
they?"

Ships were exploding, burning. Wreckage everywhere. Crates and
litter from broken crates, patches of fire, clothing, parachutes,
bodies. Powder smoke and steam and smoke from burning ships
moved with the breeze, piled up, moved again. The smoke was
sticky. The air was. Stinging. Sometimes the smoke coagulated into
islands, and ships moved into them for places to hide, but the wind,
stronger now, pushed the smoke away each time and the ships were
exposed again, the bombers still there.

The *Centaur* was on fire. Arnold, Rand, the Stacks, all the others,
were working to get it put out. They were using firefoam, and hoses
fitted with fog nozzles. It had not got to the tanks yet. A deck fire. A
big one. When the tanks went, the whole ship would go. The fire was

forcing people towards the bow. They kept backing away from it. It was getting bigger, and they were dropping their hoses and running. There was nowhere to run, except overboard, and they were jumping over by twos and threes and bunches.

Arnold and Kiwi and Dorrance and Tucker Vance were the only ones still trying to get it put out. They were backed against the rail now. The rail was hot, and the deck was.

Leonard Norris was wheelman. He took his right hand off the wheel for long enough to cross himself. Then, holding the wheel manfully, and having consigned himself to what there might be for him of mercy and justice, Leonard turned the ship into the wind, so that the wind moved the fire away from the front of the ship. He thought he recognized some of the people down there. The fire heaved in a cloud towards the bridge, and the Mate, Courtney, took off.

People were able to get at the Fire Control Points then. They got the fire under control, and they were getting it put out. The ship stayed headed into the wind for a few minutes. By the time it changed course again, they had the fire out. The ship changed direction again. Nobody was handling the wheel, and it was wandering.

Kiwi, Larry Stack, Arnold, got to the wheelhouse. Norris was flopping around on the deck up there. The glass around the wheelhouse was shattered, and the paint on the metal frames was burned away. The spokes of the wheel were scorched. Pieces of burned skin and flesh were sticking to them. People had to keep moving. The deck was too hot for them to stand in one place. While they were lifting their feet up and down, Leonard got still, and then he was dead.

A day. Another one. Yet a third one, with no planes at all. Even the Condors were gone. By that time, what remained of the convoy, thirteen ships and two DE's, was bearing south. They were around the bend now, the Cape, and they were nearing port.

Arnold was off duty. He had taken the burn ointment off his face this morning. He had been wearing sulfadiazine and white tannic acid paste. Luks and Dorrance and Vance had been. The fire had got close to them. It had blistered their faces.

Wylie Dorrance came in. He came over and sat down by Arnold. He nodded, and Arnold nodded back to him. He had, finally, not run. It had in fact happened that he didn't run. He wanted to say something about it to Arnold. Then he didn't want to. There was no need to. Besides, Arnold already knew.

Larry Stack came in. Kiwi, some others. Stack's brother was in sickbay, with a broken shoulder. Larry wanted to take a tray of food to him, but Caskie the steward said would he wait a little. Chow was not ready yet.

"You guys ought to be in a show or something," Larry Stack said. "You should been wearing that stuff on your faces before. You could just scared them planes off, kid. Couldn't you? Who's your make-up man anyway, kid?"

"You talking to Chancellor?" Kiwi said. "You know what his name is?"

"Why—sure. I know the man's name, Luks. I'm proud to know his name."

"Then how about calling him by his name? He don't go by the name kid. He signed on as Chancellor, okay?"

"All right, Luks, all right. You don't have to go jumping all over anybody, do you?"

By next week, the days would be getting longer again. By the week after that, they might be enough longer that it could be noticed. By the end of the month, next month, it would be easy to tell they were longer.

Still snowing. Easy and thick and steady, continuing. For many hours now. From back in the afternoon sometime. From before that. Days now, off and on, snowing.

Down in the mountains, the snow would be deep. Drifted.

What time now. And after a time he lifted his arm.

His left arm was still clumsy to work. He had lifted it too high. The cast had been taken off several days back, but without the weight of the cast, the muscles still did more than he wanted them to. Omega watch. Second hand. Minute hand. Hour hand. Three-eighteen a.m. Many hours now, snowing.

That was good luck about the time. Whenever it got past three
a.m. maybe he could get through the rest of it.

What day. Friday. Probably it was. Close enough. He did not need
anymore to know exactly the day. In the ship he had needed to, all of
them had, the condition of not being certain had been unbearable.
But now, no great matter.

Afterwhile he might go outside again. Up the street, toward the
train station, there was a place that stayed open all night. He could
see its sign. CAFE. Peaceful, blue. And the snow, that floated past
the window of his room. Through the blue and quiet neon glow.

He had been in that place last night. Maybe he had. Maybe he had
only been dreaming. Dreams had all kinds of details sometimes.
That was no great matter either. If he had been dreaming. If he had
not.

If he had found himself a room in a good hotel, he would not need
to go out on the street anytime. Food could be sent to the room.
Denise Houston had offered to let him stay in her apartment. It was
a hotel he wanted, though, at any rate a place entirely his own while
he had it. Somewhere he could hole up, take cover, and a crummy
hotel, this one, felt like the right place.

Denise Houston had told him he should go directly home. She had
said it twice. And said then that if he would tell her how to get in
touch with his family, she would do that. Maybe it had got through
to her that the thing to do was let it be.

He had seen lately that what he ought to do was to get another
ship. In a few days, go on over to the hall. Tomorrow. Sign on again.
Another tanker. Or anything that was on the board.

Train station. Grand Central. It was four blocks up the street
from here. Somebody had said that was not the right one. Denise. It
was Denise who had said that. She had told him he could get a train
at the Pennsylvania Station. That was the one that had the trains
down to where he lived. The mountains.

Neither one. He had seen Denise, as he had promised Kiwi he
would, and that had been enough. Before that, he had gone to see a
priest, since he had said he would do that, and told him what Kiwi
had wanted told. "Don't forget, Chancellor, okay? Raise your right

hand." And when both things were done, he had come to this hotel. If he could have done any more, he would have. He had realized, though, before too late, that he had done all he had it in him to do.

If Kiwi had only made it, maybe things would be different.

Right. Sure thing. They were only going to be the way they were.

The ships had been six days at Murmansk. What with the unloading, there had not been any resting time. The people off the *Centaur* had been able to get ashore for part of one afternoon, though.

They had gone to a building called the Arctic Hotel. Two guards had been along all the time. The streets had pits and craters, from bombings. Many wrecked buildings. Nearly every intersection had a concrete statue of Stalin.

The street-level front of the hotel was boarded over. It had been bombed. Murmansk had been bombed many times. The lobby and lunchroom in the hotel were crowded. People were drinking vodka and tea, and they were eating bread and what turned out to be Spam. The men off the *Centaur* were being stared at. Some of them had bandages and splints, but a good number of the Russians also had bandages, crutches, empty sleeves.

Fifteen or twenty of the Russians, Army people, were gathered around a big table. Two of them, sort of young, big and husky-looking, came over. One of them said something the *Centaur* people could not make out at first. He said it again, slow. "Comrade Sailors." Stack said something to them. It was Russian, but he too had to say it twice. When the soldiers understood him they smiled, big, and shook hands with him, and pulled two chairs over and sat down. Arnold wanted to know what Stack had said, and Stack told him and the others he had said Sit down and have a drink with us.

Some more vodka was on the way. One of the soldiers had got up again and gone to the bar for it. The shelves at the bar were nearly empty. Liquor was scarce. Luks had brought some brandy with him, though. He offered it to the soldiers, and one of them sampled it and closed his eyes and said Da, Da, and the other one sampled it and did the same thing. Three or four of the people off the ship had whisky, and what with that, and the vodka, there was enough. The soldiers knew enough English, and Stack could manage enough Russian, that they could communicate. The soldiers were in an anti-aircraft outfit. Luks told them, through Stack, that part of the deck cargo on the *Centaur* was anti-aircraft ammunition, and when they understood, one of them poured some vodka for Luks and handed it to him, and spoke to Stack again. "He says they'll know what to do with it," Stack said. "He said they proceed their thanks."

"They do what to their thanks?"

"They proceed them. I know it don't sound right, but it's the best I can do."

"Well, tell them we proceed ours."

Stack told them, and there was more vodka-pouring and brandy-pouring and whisky-pouring, and Stack was busy trying to tell people what was being said.

None of the people in the room looked desperate. They were of all ages, some of them elderly, some of them younger than Arnold, but even though they had been bombed and bombed and bombed and still had their backs to the wall, they looked as if they had found out that they could even so come through with whatever the situation was going to cost them, and more. Bringing the ships in might after all turn out to count for something. It felt to Arnold as if all the people from the *Centaur* were getting the same impression.

People had gathered from several tables. More bottles appeared. And, all at once, everybody had started singing.

The singing did not last long. The Army men and the others were all too close to being exhausted, the way the men off the *Centaur* were.

Guards, Russians, were at the bottom of the gangway of each ship, all the time. To respond, Wedeck had the *Centaur* gangway raised, and assigned two men to stand watch at the top of it. Wedeck was Ship's Master now. He was a First Mate, technically, but command had come to him when the Captain they had started with was killed. The Captain, Swicker, had been buried at sea. There had been several such burials.

Wedeck met the two port officials when they came on board. Twelve or fifteen other people, their staff and bodyguards, were with them. They came on once when the tanks were being discharged, and a second time to take delivery of the deck cargo. Wedeck was outnumbered. The second time, however, he put on full uniform, with braid on his cap and gold bands on his sleeves and medals for being torpedoed and for other things on the front of his coat. He was going to lend one to Kiwi, since Kiwi had been Acting Third Mate since the first week of the trip. Instead, Kiwi got a civilian suit out of his belongings. It was a blue one, Brooks Brothers. Everett Lessing pressed it for him. Wedeck said it was probably the first Brooks suit that had been worn in Murmansk, USSR. The port officials that time spoke to Kiwi first, and Kiwi indicated to them that Wedeck was the man. Courtney looked pouty, but the other three of them were heavy, and sharp-looking, and Wedeck that time held his own.

Some of the deck crates had refrigerators, and they turned out to be the wrong kind. They were Kelvinators, and they were supposed to be Westinghouses. The receiving official kept pointing to a line on a page of some papers he had on a clipboard, and holding the board towards Wedeck's face. "Vasting yotses, vasting yotses." Stack was nearby, and there was also an interpreter, but it was still hard to tell what the receiving official was saying, until he tried once again and said, slowly, "Vesting outsos." Wedeck told him finally, Take it or leave it. The interpreter translated. The official stamped, and walked away. His staff joined him, and the group of them talked for several minutes. They came on back then, and accepted the Kelvinators.

The receiving officials were maybe more alarmed than angry. They had signed for cargo that had not been ordered, and now they would need to explain to somebody over them what they had done. They were different from the men in the Arctic Hotel. Tobin said they were the same type as the ones that had wanted his friend Simmons to pay for the Coast Guard dog. "There's some types of people that it's just hard to get away from."

The ships left at seven one morning, late in September. Three

Russian DE-type ships went with them along the channel and into open water. The same three had escorted them the last few hours of the way in. That afternoon, the escort turned back. Next morning, their own ships made the turn west, and they were on the way home.

What went wrong might have started going wrong before then. The strain that had already happened was only now taking effect.

The crew had become sloppy. People's clothes had got smelly. The people themselves had, and some of them had dirt sores. The ship had washing machines, in the main head, but nobody was using them anymore. Relief watches were sometimes late, before long usually late, and people on the relief watch and the watch going off were bitching at each other.

The wheelhouse was cold. All the wheelhouse windows had been ruined, in the fire, and there had only been plywood and glass from doors to replace them with. Wind came through the cracks now. People stuffed wiper rags into the leaks. Courtney ordered the stuffing taken out. He had not objected to it, before. Now he said it made the wheelhouse look un-shipshape. "This vessel is going to be shipshape, and no backtalk. Do I make myself clear?"

Wedeck overruled him. Courtney took out his resentment on Larry Stack and various others. Stack told him to go to hell. Courtney ordered him to his quarters, and told him he would be docked his pay for that watch.

"Fuck that noise, old buddy."

"I also expect to be called Mister Courtney, not old buddy."

"You know what you can do with what you expect?"

Stack and three others, by-passing Kiwi, went to Wedeck and told him to get Courtney off their backs. Courtney came in. The situation was broken off by an Alert Alarm.

People did not move as fast for it as they had for the ones when the ships were east-bound. This particular time they did not exactly need to. There was only one plane. A slow one, an observation plane. The DE's were firing. The plane circled the convoy once, and left.

Next day another one showed up, and the same thing happened again. The ships were back in the area where they could be reached by planes from Norway.

The day after that, three fast planes arrived, and did some strafing. There was no damage to speak of. There was another strafing later that day, and the next day, two more. One for the morning, one for the afternoon.

A let-up happened when the ships met a series of rainsqualls. Sleety rain. The foul-weather gear people had did not give much protection anymore. Jackets, hoods, raintrousers, had holes, or the waterproofing had worn away. People got their gear thawed and dried, when they came off watch, but right away after they went back on it was soaked again. They tried putting lubricating oil on it, and they got varnish out of the paint locker. Neither one did much good. The oil was maybe a little better than the varnish.

People were slipping and falling a lot. Many of them already had abrasions and bruises. Places that had looked healed became raw again, and the new ones were not healing much at all. A good many of the injuries had happened after the heavy attacks had ended. Now they were happening again.

Once when a man fell he didn't bother about getting up again. Another man was with him, but the other one did not give him a hand. They were on the catwalk that had been built out over the deck cargo. The cargo was gone now, but the catwalk was still being used. It was icy. It had a safety-rail, and the man who had slipped only kept his arm crooked over it and waited, head down. After a time, he got himself, heavily, up again. Before, whoever was with a man that slipped would have helped him get up. He probably would not have slipped anyway.

When the weather cleared, the air attacks started again. The new ones were with bombers. Yet nobody rushed anymore. It took great effort, to aim the guns, undertake to work them.

Any time the weather cleared for a few hours, the planes were there. Alarms, screeching. People's first notion was to say the hell with it. They went ahead. Got to their firing stations again. A ship got sunk. Another one got damaged, and lines were rigged to it and it was towed. The next time, another one was sunk. One of the bombers was brought down. It did not matter much. There were too many bombers for the getting of just one to matter.

People were confused. Slowed down, and it took some seconds to translate sounds, words, into meaning. Motions were painful. Bending especially was. For a time, people had been careful how they spoke to each other, so as not to get anybody sore. That passed, and most of what people said was bitching at each other. That passed too. Nothing was said, except when the effort was unavoidable.

Wedeck got pneumonia. There was sulfanilamide, but it was not working right, for him. Courtney became in command, for the time being. In theory he did. He gave orders, but nobody had bothered much with him before, and they didn't now.

Walter Stack got a respiratory ailment. He was already in sickbay, with a cracked shoulder blade, and whenever he had to cough it was misery. If the ship had an epidemic, that would finally round things out. Arnold was coughing one afternoon. Dorrance said to him, "For God's sake, Chancellor, will you stop that?"

He went to sleep, sort of, in a chair in the cabin one day. Rand and Dorrance were in their bunks asleep. The three of them shared the cabin. He had thought he would do something with the navigation manual he had got from Kiwi once. At one time, Kiwi had been teaching him the use of a sextant, and had lent him the necessary book, *The American Practical Navigator*. It was an old copy, with covers that had been taped to hold them to the spine. Kiwi had written his name in it. Keyswick Harrison Luks. New York, 1934. After Arnold had the book out, though, he only let it lay on the table. If he got in his bunk he might be comfortable. It was not so bad where he was, though, and he had dozed off.

This was how it must be after somebody had had a convulsion. After a long fever. Drained. Peaceful.

By that time, somebody had come in. Two people. There was a draft, and footsteps.

Kiwi. Felix Gorman was with him. Gorman was Assistant Chief, from down in the engine room.

He put his head down again on the table.

Kiwi told him to get up and start cleaning the room. His shirt was sweaty. He probably had a fever. No matter. Okay, Chancellor. Get on your feet. If he didn't do anything, Luks and the other man would go back out. "Okay, Chancellor. Get on your feet." In the end he was standing up, and making motions about cleaning the cabin. That seemed to be what Luks wanted. Luks got Rand and Dorrance out of their bunks. When the three of them were working, more or less, Kiwi told them when they were finished with the cabin to start on the corridor. Kiwi and Gorman went to the next cabin.

An argument started in that one. It was Larry Stack's, and Stack's voice came in over Kiwi's. "Buddy, you can wind your ass around the other direction and get the hell out of here. Take that Goddamn engine room man with—." Stack did not finish. There was a different sound, an impact, and then the sound of stumbling, and then a crash.

People were gathering at the door of Stack's cabin. Inside, Stack was sprawled on the floor. Luks was standing near him, waiting. Stack got up.

"Want some more?" Luks said. "Want to go be with your brother in sickbay?"

"It ain't over, Luks. You'll get yours."

"Then let's get it over. Come on."

Eventually, Stack backed down. His roommate began picking up some of the litter. In a minute, Stack joined in. Luks and Felix Gorman went on to the next cabin. The people at the door were going away. Somebody sort of laughed. "You see old Luks deck that guy?" Goddamn, Stack weighs two hundred pounds easy. I thought we'd hit a mine or something, when I heard him drop."

The corridor had patches of dried blood. A place that looked as if somebody had puked. At one time, the corridor had been mopped every day. The walls and the overhead had been soojied once a week.

It got cleaned again, and the cabins did, and the heads. Sometimes Gorman came around to check on the work, sometimes Kiwi did. When it was getting finished, both of them came around, and gave out word that chow would not be served to anybody who was not washed up. There was muttering. It got louder. Somebody said "You sucking up to Courtney or something?" Kiwi located the group it was coming from. They subsided, and went back to work.

When he told Denise about it, she was surprised. She did not altogether believe it at first that Kiwi had knocked anybody down. That was the only time he himself had seen Kiwi lose his temper. It had not lasted that time all of thirty seconds. When Stack had got up again, and was bringing himself around to backing down, Kiwi had not crowded him, had not said anything to humiliate him. Had not said anything at all.

He was interested in how Kiwi had managed to get people to shape up again. To bring them back towards being a crew. Kiwi said he didn't know. He had had to make it up as he went along.

"I didn't do much anyway," Kiwi said. "I couldn't if I'd wanted to. I guess I did want to. But most of them would have made it anyway. On their own."

"I don't see how."

"I don't either. They would, though. But the way it was, see, you were the first one we got to. Me and Gorman. I got him in on it so he could help handle the engine people. And if you'd bucked us, Chancellor, we'd probably have quit."

"I did buck you."

Kiwi smiled. "You didn't make it stick. If you had, I think we'd have stopped without going any farther. You came through, so I thought I'd try my luck again. Stack came through pretty good himself, I guess. He mouthed off at me, and that got my adrenalin running. That way I was mad enough to get the other guys in line. I'd rather anybody would punch me than wise off at me. It does look like a lot of dramatics, though," Kiwi said. "Just to get a few floors mopped."

The planes came back again, for what turned out to be the last time. One morning, attack bombers, four of them, with machine guns, and after they had used their bombs, all the bombs misses, they came over with the guns. They only fired for a second or two, each one of them. The planes were stunting a little, rolling. It was possible they had intended for the bombs to be misses. Luks had made a run out onto the catwalk, to get a man who had been hurt out there. People thought the planes had left. But there was one more, and it cut him down. The ship's gunners got it, and it was streaming smoke as it left, but that didn't help. It had already cut him down.

"Let's go, Chancellor." That was Larry Stack. The two of them brought him in. The sickbay was filled, so they took him to his cabin. People were crowding around, wanting to help carry him, but Stack, snarling at them, would not let them. Dorrance cleared a way, and they put Luks on his bunk.

Luks needed blood, and everybody who could walk, including the Navy Armed Guard, lined up to give him some. It was an Armed Guard man he had gone out onto the catwalk for. The man had not been hurt after all. He had slipped, and only stunned himself. Nine people had the kind of blood Luks could use. Lessing was one of them. Lessing went first. Bailey the medic made it a vein-to-vein transfusion. Arnold took his shirt off, his shirt already sopping as his dungarees were with blood Luks had lost, and Bailey got another pint while the first one was going in.

Kiwi's breathing began to slow. By the time the second pint was getting finished, his breathing was sounding normal, and he was conscious again. His eyes were not focused, but he knew what was going on. Bailey gave him a third pint. He was working out of the shock-stage by then, and the pain was catching up with him. Bailey gave him an injection, to hold the pain back some.

His leg bones had too many breaks to let them be set. It would take surgery to fix them. What Bailey could do was prevent infection, and give him sedatives.

Arnold and Larry Stack and Frank Tobin took turns standing by in his cabin. Wedeck came in twice. Wedeck was getting over pneumonia, and he had to sit down when he got there. The second day, Lessing came in. Bailey was not letting many people in, but he allowed Everett Lessing for a few minutes. He told Kiwi that Lessing had been the first one to give him blood.

"That right? Thanks a lot, man."

"Don't mention it. You can do as much for me sometime."

"Thanks a lot." Kiwi smiled. "I guess that makes me a queer by transfusion, then."

"Well, Keyswick, there's more where that came from."

The next day, Bailey wanted Arnold to make another transfusion. It was dangerous to give any again so soon. Bailey had him stay on a stretcher for some time afterwards, and kept checking his pulse. Stack came in, and Bailey got some from Stack. Stack told him to make it two pints, and Bailey did. Luks was rallying again.

That afternoon, though, he was going under. Some of the men gathered in the corridor, and soon some more. Now and then Luks was struggling. Bailey had strapped his legs, and given him sedatives, but the struggling made the bone-ends move anyway, and when the pain got through, Luks would yell. One of the men in the corridor, and then another one, left. The sounds were too much for them. Arnold took something, a cloth, and wiped Kiwi's forehead with it. What there was of Kiwi looked at him. Then, though, he was gone again.

Somebody said, "It's close to four, Chancellor." He was due to go on watch at four. He thought of seeing if somebody would take his watch for him. One of the things Luks had wanted, though, and had brought about, was that people would run the ship right.

It was already dark, outside. The time of protracted daylight had been over for many weeks. There was a meteor burst. They had been happening yesterday also. George Rand has said they were from the Orionid stream. Another burst happened. Bright one. All these lifetimes, the planet had been meeting the Orionid fragments each time it got to this point of its orbit.

Luks died at ten that night. Wedeck, many others, were in his cabin and in the corridor. Luks had been asking people to give him a hand. "Get that thing off me, will you? Goddamn it, Chancellor, I thought me and you were friends. Get it off the top of me." After a time, the talking stopped. The struggling happened, or started to, but then he got still. Right away, it was all over.

Topside, there was one meteor burst after another, a new one arriving before the reflections of the one before it finished fading in the water. "Never saw them this much before," Rand said.

When this planet broke up, particles from it might afterwards make flashes for some other world.

Maybe the other one would not have so much killing.

Some of the people went on to sleep. Some of them still kept watch.

Luks would be buried when daylight came.

There was reminiscing now and then. They spoke of the times he had helped people. Of times when he had been down and had turned to people he had shipped with. Tobin, and Gorman, had made trips with him before. A number of the others, who had not actually met him, had heard of him.

"He was the best one we had," Stack said. "The best one we had."

And all that night and the next day, and all the days and nights from then on, they grieved for him, and for their other shipmates who were perished and lost.

Denise had wanted to know if things had been quick for Kiwi, at the end. He told her they had been. By the way she looked at him, however, he saw she knew better. "He had a bad time, didn't he?" she said. "I'm glad you told me he didn't, though. I appreciate it."

One of the Norwegians in the crew had been arrested by the Germans once, and in their jail he had heard people the Germans were working on in another part of it. The man said they had sounded the way Kiwi did.

Denise was pregnant. She was extremely pregnant. She was in the middle of her eighth month, she said, and it was going to be twins. If they were boys, she would name one of them Keyswick, and the other one Harrison.

"I might even give them those names if they're girls. I suppose I ought to be worrying about what their last name will be. I'd make it Luks, if I could do that legally. Ain't it awful? I'm about to have two illegitimate babies, and all I can think about is how glad I am they're his . . . Well, it isn't, of course. I mean it isn't all I can think about. All this time, you know, I felt sure he'd get back. I'd hope that if I dreamed anything, it would be about him being back again without anything happening to him. I went to church practically every day. They have this Stella Maris Church on 9th Avenue, you know. That's close by, and I'd stop in there. I really did think he'd get back."

She asked if she could get him a drink. Liquor was not something he wanted, though. She said that Luks had told her that sometimes when he first got off ships he had not been able to drink. Then she wanted to give him some supper. Eating anything, trying to, would have been labor. Still he ate most of a sandwich she made. She brought in a plateful, and he got through most of one.

When he first got back, he had thought that he did want liquor. He had trouble finding a bar that would serve him. He was underage. "You don't belong in a bar anyway, fellow. You look like you belong in some kind of hospital, if you want to know." Late one aftenoon, he was in Power's, across the street from the hall. He had been going along the streets most of the day, and when he noticed he was near the hall he went on in, and when he left, crossed over to Power's. The bartender in there had been about to turn him down, but one of the other customers told the bartender to go ahead. "Put it in front of me. Okay. You're not serving him, you're serving me." Several of the people in Power's had crutches, or arm-slings. It was like the Artic Hotel. He still had the arm-cast, at the time. The man who had spoken to the bartender had a patch over the left eye. His name was Tom Loomis. When Loomis was leaving, he spoke to one of the other customers. "See this guy here? If that bartender bastard gives him a hard time, you buy his drinks for him, okay? He'll pay for them, that's not what I mean, you just do the ordering. Take it easy, Chancellor. See you around." Liquor was not what he wanted, however. The people in here, and some of them in the hall, were easy to be around—except for Denise they were about the only ones he had seen since he got back who didn't look like they needed to be slammed into—but after the first drink and part of another one he went on outside again.

Denise thought the arm-crack was from something serious. It was only from a fall, though. The day before the ships reached Reykjavik again, he had slipped, and fractured the small bone in his left forearm. It was only a crack, Bailey said, instead of a break.

He stayed long enough in her apartment to make sure she did not need any money. He had been fairly sure from the first, by the looks of her apartment. It was not luxurious, but it would make a good place to live. She had been working, she said, up until six weeks ago. She been one of the farm girls in *How Now Brown Cow*. After she became too pregnant, she got some radio parts. For them, appearance hadn't mattered so much. Since back in November, though, she had not been working at all. She didn't want to be taking any needless chances. Luks had arranged for monthly checks to be sent to her, but she had been able to keep all of them in the bank. Luks had a considerable amount of insurance, and he told her that Luks had written a will, and Wedeck and Tobin had witnessed it, to have the insurance go to her.

"Arnold? Would you—like to have something of his? Several of his things are here."

"He gave me this watch, Denise." He showed her the Omega. Kiwi had taken it off, during one of the times he was clear in his head, and told him to keep it. Kiwi had said, "And then when you get home—." But he hadn't finished.

"Yes. That is his. Was his. I remember it now. I'm glad he did."

She had invited him to come back. He had said Thank you, but he thought both of them understood he would not be back. Not soon. Maybe not at all.

None of the crew had wanted to stick with each other, after ship got to port. All of them had gone different ways.

When he left her apartment was when it had started snowing. Three days ago now. It had kept snowing, off and on, since then.

The day before the ships turned south, towards Iceland and Reyk-javik again, a plane had met them. A B-24. Long-range patrol plane. Blue and white, Navy plane, and the thing he had thought of, when he saw it, was the Dove that had come back to the Ark. The flood was ending, and a dove had returned. People had gone to their gun stations when they heard the plane. Then it came in sight, and by that time they realized they had not needed to.

They had done odd things when they realized they were going to be safe again. One man had kept punching his fist against a wall. Larry Stack went to the sickbay, to tell his brother things were going to be okay now, but when he got there he could not say anything. He only sat by Walter Stack's bunk for a while, shaking.

What remained of the convoy stayed two weeks at Reykjavik. Many people were taken off the ships. The Navy base had a hospital. One of the Navy corpsmen looked at the *Centaur* and at the people who were staying on, and said Good Godamighty. Tobin got off, at Reykjavik. He had flu. Walter Stack got off, because of his cracked shoulder. He and Larry were twins, and Larry arranged to get off with him.

If the convoy had been completely smashed, things would have been simple. If only there had not been anything left, nothing now would need to be done. Something had been left, though. It was not possible yet, to rest.

In a way, Luks had it made. Not in a way. He actually did. Luks was out of it, now. And others were. Many. They were clear. They themselves were fully at rest.

He had heard his father say something once. Where they lived was in the mountains, by a creek. There had been a flood, and his father had said, "I wish to God it had took everything." His mother had said to stop talking like that in front of the chldren. What his father meant, he saw later, and again now, was that if the flood had in fact taken everything, it would not be necessary to try anymore.

As things were, it was necessary. There was another thing his father had said. Stay with it.

Zipper bag. Clothes. To put his clothes in it.

He had been to Murmansk and back, with only a zipper canvas bag for luggage.

There would not be any getting completely back. Once you went out far enough, you had to forget about getting much of the way back.

That was the reason, for going out at all. Part of the reason.

Because of the waters of the flood.

He would not get another ship immediately. To let this trip get a little more finished first. Get home for a while, and then get another one. The trips would still be here. Waiting for somebody to make them. It would not do to keep them waiting too long, but still. Back and forth. That was what things were going to come to. That was all they had come to. A lot of going back and forth. Murmansk. Anywhere else.

Train station. The one that had the trains down to the mountains. Get up. Get started.

He would need to walk to it. This time of the day, four a.m., something like that, there would not be any taxis. The snow besides. Still falling. No tire tracks in it yet. No footprints.

Then he would walk. Through the snow, and to the station. And by tonight, he could be down there. In only that much time now, he could be home.

Down by the Riverside

Glenn Stoneman was standing at the gate of his yard when Mike came along. Mike thought Glenn knew him. Glenn did not wave back, though, when Mike waved. Mike said Hi, but Glenn did not answer.

When he was nearly past Glenn's yeard, Glenn did say something. "Your grass ain't cut."

He stopped. The grass in their yard was in fact long. He wondered when Glenn had seen it. They only lived three blocks from each other, but Glenn had not been by their house any time he knew of.

"Ours is cut," Glenn said. "You think it looks nice?"

"Your yard? I guess so. Sure."

"I know it does. Our yard looks nice all the time."

Glenn was smiling. It looked like he knew something secret. He smiled that way at school. They were both in the third grade, and the people Glenn spent time with at school would look at each other sometimes, and smile together.

"Your old man couldn't cut the grass if he wanted to," Glenn said. "You got a one-legged old man, you know it?"

His father had a peg leg. Prosthesis. Once when his father was buckling it on, his father said This thing is going to come unbolted some day and I'm going to fall on my Goddamn rear end. "If you'll take me with you I'll help you get up again." When he said that, his father looked at him. He started getting nervous. His father had hit him sometimes when he first got out of the war. But it turned out all right. "Sure, Michael. We'll do that."

"My dad says your old man's a really tough bastard, though," Glenn said. "My dad regards your old man a lot. He regards everybody that was in combat. He said even if your old man does have all that education he's still a tough bastard. He said they ought to went ahead and gave him the Congreshal." Glenn whistled. "Congressional. Yeah. Hard to say that word, you know it? Medal of Honor, while they were at it."

Mike wanted to get where he was going. He had it in mind to go over to West End Avenue and get himself a soda. He was probably not supposed to be out of his yard. He knew he was not. His father and mother were not home yet, but the housekeeper was there. He had not got permission from her.

"Well—see you later, Glenn."

"Not if I see you first, liverwurst. That's what my dad says to me sometimes. When he's leaving to go to work, or go to the tavern or something? He talks to me like I'm equal to him, a lot of the time. Where you going, anyway? Mind if I go with you?"

"I don't mind. Come on."

Glenn held back. "My dad and mother ain't home yet. Are yours?"

"Not yet."

"They both work too, huh?"

"My mother does. My father hasn't found anything he wants yet."

"Can't get work, huh? That's a bad break, Mike. My dad says lots of people are getting laid off now. That's bad. Your mother makes enough to keep you going, though, right? That's better than nothing. My dad does have a job already. I mean I'm pretty sure he does. He got his job as soon as he got out of uniform. He puts electric wires in houses. And every other night he goes to electric welding institute. The Veterans pays for it, how about that? He'll make really good money when he finishes with that. He makes enough now, but he wants to better himself. So I'll have things better than he did, you know what I mean? Welders don't ever get laid off. That's where he is now, at work. Maybe my mother went to meet him. I bet that's where she is. She went—. She never does that, though. I don't give a damn where she is, frankly. Maybe she's shacked up with some son of a bitch somewhere. I can't stand people that shack up with somebody when they're still married to their husband, can you? My dad sure can't. He said he can't. If I caught anybody doing that, I'd shoot him like a dog. I already know where my dad keeps his pistol. He said he'd give me a fat lip if I touched it, but I would if I had to." Glenn took one of his pistols out of its holster and pointed it towards him. Glenn had a pair. "Where you want it, you red Commie? Head or guts?" He lowered the pistol. "You want to wear one of these, Mike? What's the matter?"

"You sure were talking."

Glenn smiled. "I was, I guess. My dad says I talk like a jaybird sometimes. You want to wear one of these?"

"Sure. I'll try one."

Glenn unhooked the holster for the pistol, and gave it to him. "Here. Don't have any caps for them, but it don't matter."

Mike put the holster on his own belt. Got his belt and pants settled on him again, and patted the holster. Once he had had a pistol of his own, that could take a full roll of caps. He had lost it. After his father got back, he had asked for a new one, but his father said No. Too many guns already.

"Where you want to go, Glenn?"

"Anyplace. You name it."

"West End Avenue, okay?"

"Where? That's a hundred blocks."

It was only eight blocks. Maybe Glenn still wouldn't go. Maybe the housekeeper would notice he was not around, and start calling him. That way, he could go on back home.

"I'm ready if you are, though, Mike. Anyplace is fine by me."

They went to the Westway Grocery Shop. It was more of a candy store than a grocery, and they got Pepsi Colas, and potato chips. There was a bench out front. They sat down.

"What's your full name, Mike?"

"Michael Turner Todd Reeves."

"You got four names? You must be named after a lot of people, all right. Who were you named after?"

"I had this uncle named Michael, that got killed in the war. He was my father's brother, see. That's the first two parts. Because his middle name was Turner. And then I have this grandfather and his name is Todd Reeves."

"You had an uncle that got killed? And your father got wounded besides? You really come from a tough family. You like to know my full name? Gable Glenn Stoneman. That's the reason I asked you what yours is, see. So I could tell you mine. You like to know who I was named after? Clark Gable, and Glenn Ford."

"Are they your uncles or something?"

"No, man. Clark Gable's in the movies, don't you know anything? Glenn Ford too. What my mother did, see, she took one name from each one of them, and she put the two names together. She said if I'd turned out to be a girl she was going to name me Madeline. Ain't that some shit? They have this woman in the movies named Madeline somebody. Madeline Carroll. My dad calls her Madeline Car-roll. And my mom had the name picked out already. I'm sure glad I wasn't a girl. I wouldn't mind having a sister, but as for being a girl myself, I couldn't take it. You don't have any brothers or sisters either, do you Mike?"

"Not yet. Maybe next year I will. My father took all the seeds with him, see, when he went overseas."

"What seeds?"

"The ones for babies. He fixed me up, see, but then he was gone. I guess I will now, since he's back. They already said I might."

"Mike, that's the worst thing I ever heard. They don't make babies with seeds."

"What do they do it with, then?"

"I tell you, Mike. If you don't know, you better just find out."

"My father said it comes from seeds. He ought to know."

"I still say it's crap."

"Say anything you want to. I don't care."

"Anything I want to, huh."

"Sure. Glenn? What are you looking at me like that for?"

"I'm not looking at you any way. But that's what my mother says to my dad sometimes."

"What is?"

"Say anything you want to. When he finds out she's been shacking—. I mean . . ."

Most of the Pepsi Cola was gone. He finished what was left of it. Glenn had already finished his. They had some chips left, but they could take those along.

"You ready to go back, Glenn?"

Glenn shook his head.

"You want another soda, then? I still got a quarter and a dime left. I can get us one."

Glenn shook his head.

"I'll get me one, then. What are you crying about, Glenn?"

"Who the hell's crying?"

"You are. You were. I thought you were."

"Well I wasn't."

"Oh. Okay, then. I'm going to get me another one."

"He doesn't treat me like I'm equal to him. He don't even treat me like I'm his. He got loaded up one night and when he came in he said somebody else knocked her up while he was away."

In a minute, he went on into the store.

He got ginger ale this time, for variety. He got two bottles, in case Glenn wanted one anyway. He was going to get some candy, but he saw on the shelf back of the candy counter some pistol caps, and he got two roll of caps instead.

Glenn was looking mean, instead of like he was crying, when he got back. Glenn smiled, though, when he gave him the ginger ale. "Hey. Thanks a lot, pal."

He took the rolls of caps out of his pocket.

"Hey. Man, you really are a friend. You get these just now? Man, we'll shoot up the Goddamn town."

A street bus went by.

"Mike. Listen, let's go pay a visit to my grandfather. He don't live far. It's in the country, but the bus goes most of the way. Like that one that just went by? We take it to the end of the line, and then we walk a little way, and that's it. I know the way good. Come on."

He hadn't thought Glenn would come up with anything like this.

"Come on, Mike. It only costs fifteen cents. I got two more dimes. I didn't tell you, but I do. You got bus fare, don't you? Come on, okay? Okay, Seeds? Okay?"

Dusty dark, now. Six-thirty. He could still make out shapes, if they were moving, but that was all.

Light thickens, and the crows wing home to the rook-filled wood. Something like that. It was in Macbeth.

John, it says The crow makes wing to the rooky wood.

That was his brother speaking to him. Mike.

Makes wing to the rooky wood. And night's black agents to their preys do rouse.

Kids disappeared. The paper last spring had something about a kid who disappeared out of a supermarket, in the middle of the afternoon. His mother had realized he was not with her when she was in the aisle that had dry cereals. She turned around to ask him what kind he wanted, and he was not there. He had not been found.

Take it easy, John. Just relax.

Yes. If he panicked, that would be the thing not to do.

It was probably what he wanted to do. It would put him out of commission, and then somebody else would need to handle the situation.

Mike had not been in the house when he got home. That was at four-thirty. The housekeeper said Mike had got in from school at the regular time. Three o'clock. He had changed his clothes, and she had given him two sandwiches. He had taken them out to the backyard. He had wanted another one. She had it already fixed, just in case. Then, a little after four, she had noticed he was not around. She had called for him, and gone looking for him. "The next thing I was going to do, Mr. Reeves, was get your wife on the phone. I would have got you on the phone, of course, but I didn't know where to get in touch with you." She was upset bad. He had seen as soon as he came in that something was wrong.

She knew what kind of clothes Mike had put on. When he was talking to the police, he was able to tell them how Mike had been dressed. And after that, he telephoned Rachel, at her office. It was nearly five by then. She was already getting ready to leave.

When she got home, the housekeeper, Mrs. Collier, told her all the details. Mrs. Collier had gone through them twice for him. Repeating the details eased her mind, but only for a while, and then she needed to repeat them again. He had told her, and Rachel had, that she was not to blame. It became clear to her eventually that they meant it. She went ahead then and went home.

He was the one that was to blame. He had told Mrs. Collier he would be back by three-thirty. He was late, and by the time he got here, Mike was gone.

He and Rachel went looking for him. Rachel kept calling. The sound was different from when women were just calling their kids to the house. It was a distress call. He had never heard it before, but he knew at once what it was. Mike would have known too, and answered, if he could have, and Mike had never heard it before. He himself wanted to answer. But he was not the one she was calling.

The neighborhood did not have many houses. People they met only said No. "Afraid not." "Sure haven't." Nobody wanted to get involved. He and Rachel had gone on back in, finally. It was getting dark by then. He had telephoned the police station again, but there was still no word. He was outside again now, in case Mike even now showed up.

To go on in. There was no need to leave Rachel by herself.

When he turned, he stumbled. After all this time, the peg leg was still hard to manage sometimes.

It was the worry about Mike that had made him clumsy.

Don't blame that kid if you can't work your equipment, John. You've had time to learn how.

Rachel had come out onto the porch. Maybe the police had found out something.

But she was only telling him to come and get some supper.

She had already put it on the table. Things had to be done. Meals got ready, places set. Scoff up. That was something his brother used to say, at meal times.

Ghosting. That was what it was called. Four years now. He was out in the islands when it started, and the squadron was making three missions a week. Mon.-Wed.-Fri. A good dependable schedule. You could plan your activities around it. Usually they did three cities a week. Sometimes they did the same city twice. Mike had been in the Navy, on an air-sea rescue boat for when planes crashed at sea. *Rest easy about me, John. It was quick, for all of us. So it's okay.* The boat Mike was on had been lost in that general area, no survivors, six months before he himself went out there. *Not boats, John. Ships. They're ships, all right?*

What had bothered him for a time was whether he was keeping Mike from his own rest. He might not be letting Mike have his death even though Mike had paid for it. That time went away. The island he was on was a small one. Nearly level. You could not walk far in any direction without arriving at the edge of it. Then the ocean. Sunrises, mild and muted and immense. Sunsets, usually rather brighter, still not spectacular. A sort of beautiful place. One man talked about putting up a vacation resort here after the war.

He had stopped having friends anymore, and so whenever somebody he knew got killed, it was, to him personally, nothing major. He could remember when it would tear him up, somebody getting killed. What had been required at those times was to pack the man's belongings in a duffel bag, for eventual shipment home. Every garment and object had to be listed and included. Lighters and cartons of cigarettes. Unfinished boxes of Hershey bars, chessboards, hunting knives, books, bundles of letters. Debris and debris. The packing was something people were reluctant about doing. He had come not to mind it. A couple of times, people asked him to take over for them, and he had. One man had had some dirty photographs. Every item was supposed to be sent back, but he and the others doing the packing that time had decided against including the photographs. It would not do for the man's family to see that stuff. Later, they made a special fire, and burned it. The same man had had a Dick Tracy BigLittle book, a comic book, that he had got when he was a kid. Debris. He himself had brought some arrowheads out there with him. They were the kind some of the Cumberland Valley people had made. Maybe some of his ancestors had. And debris. No trouble anymore getting to sleep at night. Or in the daytime, if it was day-time when the planes got back. The ones that did get back. People on the crews could be issued phenobarbital if they wanted any, whis-ky if that was what they wanted, but he never wanted either one any-more. Chaplains blessed the airplanes for each flight. One of them would also bless the bombs. The five-hundred-pounders and the two-fifties and the fire-bombs.

He had not told her about the ghosting. It was probably not any-thing so unusual, though. The one person he had said anything about it to was Reeves McCullers, after McCullers had spoken of it in connection with people McCullers had known in France and Germany.

When he was in the Atlanta hospital a couple of years ago, Reeves would visit some people there. They had got acquainted mainly be-cause of the coincidence of their names. Once they had talked about the possibility of an actual family connection, but if there was any, it was remote. His own family, his father's people, came from around Chattanooga, and McCullers was from southern Alabama.

In the hospital, the only people he had been willing to go through having anything to do with were the other amputees, and not too much of that. Reeves himself had been in bad combat, ground, and he was coming to the hospital to visit a couple of fellows who had been in his outfit. He had thought at first that McCullers was only another sightseer. Later he was curious how he could have been that mistaken. He did not want people to be looking at him. It was the same way with all of them, but it turned out that it was okay for Reeves to be there. There was not anything to notice about Reeves, other than that he was a little short, and he didn't do or say anything unusual other than visit his Army friends at all, but there was the feeling when he was around that something out of the ordinary, not necessarily pleasant but still valuable, was getting ready to happen, or had recently finished happening. When he said something of that to one of the people Reeves came to see, a man who had lost both feet and the left hand, the man said Well, when I was around him the Invasion of Normandy happened. Another man said, "I drawed to an inside straight playing poker with the little bastard once, and durn if I didn't fill it." The other man said You call your commanding officer a little bastard? and the man who played poker said I shore do. Reeves had the rank of Captain. That surprised him.

For a long time, he had left his ward only when he had to, and he had stayed as much as possible in his own neighborhood of it. There was fear of having to see different walls, faces he was not used to. He had some Cherokee blood, through his father's line, and one day, fear, he found he had been whispering Grandfather Sequoia. Grandfather Sequoia. One afternoon, though, he decided to go to the recreation room. McCullers had made four or five visits, by then. It happened that Reeves came in again. He was out in the corridor, in his wheelchair, working slow, careful, even though the corridor did not have much traffic, and Reeves said "Where to, Kilroy?" and took hold of the handles of the wheelchair and rolled him along, and they went on to the recreation room, where the others were.

He had been thinking that it might be him, not Mike, who was the ghost, and there was something that would come to mind sometimes. Ghost. Go back, ghost. Go away and leave the live people alone. But that was over with, and the unwillingness to see anything besides known walls and angles was over with. A couple of times he had talked too much. For several minutes he had not been able to stop. McCullers had been amused about it, and when he wanted to know why, McCullers said Jack, you sure were talking. He admitted it, since he could not very well deny it. Reeves said it had happened to him once, in a bar in Paris. Reeves had started talking to the bartender, or towards the bartender. The town in Alabama that McCullers came from was named Wetumpka, and he had started conjugating it for a verb. I tumpka, you tumpka, he tumpkas. Wetumpka, you tumpka, they tumpka. He had got into the perfect passive before he could quit. The bartender had not paid any attention to him. The other customers, GI's, had not paid any attention either. In Paris, in 1944, it took more than somebody running on in a bar to attract any notice.

McCullers had remarked once that maybe instead of Homo

sapiens, it ought to be Homo homicidens. If the species ever did die
out, it would be from self-inflicted wounds.

That spring, Reeves came to the hospital one last time. He was going up to New York, he said. His wife was a writer, and she was already up there. He himself would be getting out of the hospital soon.
He had been out once already, and had to come back in, but this
time he would be out for good. They shook hands, and McCullers
said God bless you, man. You'll make it now, right?

Rachel might be interested in knowing about the ghosting. She
might just think he was psycho.

She poured more coffee for them. "Did you see your mail, John?"

Some kind of circular. Taber Associates, Inc. Your Personnel
Consultants. That was an employment agency he had gone to back
in the summer, when he had had some notion of getting a job. A
printed form in the envelope. Good morning, Sir. When did you last
ask yourself What does the future hold for me? Am I making my
family as happy as I could? Who am I really?

Good questions. Real good ones.

He would not get any job for a while yet. She wanted him to get
one soon, and that was the reason she had called his attention to the
circular. He was in the lucky position of not needing to get a job.
Rachel was working because she wanted to work. She was three
months pregnant, and later in the year she would need to go on ma-
ternity leave, but there would still be sufficient.

He had been surprised, they both had, that she had not become
pregnant long back. When he was first out, there had been pressure,
with him anyway, about sex. Nothing permanent had come from any
of it, in any personal way. He had thought something would. One
man on the island had said, When I get back and get to be with my
wife again, it's going to be Christmas all the time. Later they had
needed to gather the man's belongings and put them in a duffel bag.

Working was the only thing they had ever had any actual disagree-
ment about. She believed that work was a good thing in itself. To
him, it was something to do only if you couldn't get out of it. He did
not know beyond any doubt if he could in fact hold a job yet, since he
had found out that he had to make an effort to keep his mind from

going from subject to subject, but he was not greatly worried about it. Somebody he had known overseas, the one who had talked about a vacation resort on the island, had developed a way of making rainbow popcorn. The corn was sprayed with chemicals, and the heat when it was popped brought out pastel colors. The man had wanted him to join the company. The ones who had were on the way to being rich. His idea was that anything he might get into would only be some sort of tinted popcorn. Rachel insisted that things were not that way.

It would probably be politics, whenever he did begin with something. If he was in fact off his rocker, in politics it would not show. His uncle, his mother's brother, thought that politics was something that mattered. His uncle, Mike Conagle, was not himself a politician, but he was a man of property, and politicians visited him sometimes. He had met one of them, Cordell Hull, when he was spending a week at his uncle's farm last year. The farm, an estate if his uncle had been a pretentious man, was over near the town of Carthage, east of Nashville, and that was the section Cordell Hull came from.

He had gone to sleep on the veranda that afternoon. He became awake, and an elderly man was in a chair nearby. The man smiled, quietly, and said to him, Good afternoon, Sergeant. Then his uncle introduced them. "Judge Hull, this is my nephew, Jack Reeves." He was in process of getting up—he had located his cane and taken hold of it—to shake hands, and the man told him not to get up. He did anyway, and when they shook hands, the man also bowed. It was still a minute before he realized that "Judge Hull" was Cordell Hull. Former Secretary of State. And also, last year, maybe year before last, Hull had been awarded the Nobel Peace Prize. It was year before last. The year of the atom bombings. He had wondered if Hull had had any advance information about the bomb. It felt unlikely. Yet the way things went, giving an atom bomb participant a Peace Medal made as much sense as anything else did.

Hull had asked him that afternoon, "Have you ever considered public service, Sergeant Reeves? Or am I putting beans in your nose?" His uncle said later that that could have been taken as an invitation.

He had heard people argue that the ships had been collected at Pearl Harbor so as to be bait for the Japanese. The move had worked rather too well, but it had worked. And the resulting uproar had been what was needed to get the red ants mad at the black ants. And certainly he had been one of the maddest. He had been at the recruiting station the next morning, waiting for the door to open. His brother had been there with him. Only to keep him company, since at that point Mike was not old enough to go. As far as he could see, though, the main argument against all that, the idea of the ships being used as a lure, was that the idea made sense. The way things actually happened didn't. What happened was such things as the Western Union messenger dashing around Honolulu the afternoon of December 7th trying to deliver a telegram to some admiral or general or corporal or pfc that something might be about to happen, Armageddon or something, so be careful now, you hear. They had thought it would be a good idea to send a warning that an attack was probably coming, but their radio system was out of order and they fell back on Western Union.

Conversation on the veranda, about public service, government, alternatives. It seemed to him that governments were always having wars. Whenever they could, anyway. Hull said it was only when they could not keep peace, and he said there was a difference. "That's some of the reason, Mr. Reeves, I'm hoping that men of your experience and generation will not withold your help in these matters." Déjà vu. Hundreds on hundreds of times, wars ended, elders had talked with people who were back. On verandas, under tents, by broken colonnades. His great-grandfather, a Confederate Major, the person he was named after, must have heard some such words after Appomattox. For that man, the Civil War was the war. For his uncle, it had been the First World War.

Yet what if Hull had the right idea. That—

Steps on the porch. Heavy ones. The police. They had found out something. Knocking. "Reeves? Fellow named John Reeves live here?"

Somebody in civilian clothes. He had seen the man once or twice, but he did not know his name.

"How you doing? You John Reeves? Stoneman's the name, sir. We ain't ever met, sir, but we're neighbors. I'm Glenn Stoneman's daddy. I guess your boy and mine got a little carried away with theirselves today."

Both boys were at Glenn's grandfather's house. Stoneman said when they were driving out that Glenn sometimes talked about going there. Once he had run off, and that was where he had gone. "Boy's not exactly happy at his home," Stoneman said. "Can't say I blame him much, certain conditions being what they are. Going to make me a few changes, some time not too far off." Stoneman had been later than usual getting home tonight. Nobody was around, and when Glenn was not outdoors anywhere either, he had got an idea where Glenn had gone. "I'm going to give that little monkey's ass something to make him know better the next time, if you'll excuse my language." When he telephoned his father, Glenn's grandfather, he found that another kid was there too. "Turned out to be yours. Ain't that something now. Couple of durn kids, making us go through all this. I could see this guy was a worried man, Mrs. Reeves. When the man gets to the door before the mother does, and it's a missing kid, you know he's got to be worried. Specially when he's crippled at that, can't—. Jesus, I didn't mean that the way it sounded. I'm sorry, sir. I'm sincerely sorry."

He told Stoneman it was all right. He was curious that Stoneman realized he might have been bothered by it. At one time, he would have. That long time ago.

"I apologize to you too, Mrs. Reeves. I know both of you were worried about your kid. Sure. This car's a nice-riding automobile, sir. Been driving it long?"

They talked about cars for a while. Stoneman wanted to talk, since he had been worried about his own kid, and cars were a safe subject. When Stoneman got to where he would be in a position to get a new car, he was going to get a good heavy one. Right now, he was not driving anything. He had got laid off his regular job last month. He had been with a building contractor, but construction got slow. He was working now for a meat-preparing company, where they cured hams and so on. The pay was not entirely what it ought to be, so he had sold his car. Not a bad little car, while he had it. Brakes worked fine, tires in good shape. This slow time with him was only temporary, of course. He was still going to trade school, every class he was scheduled for. He was taking up electric welding. One of the main things he had in mind was for his son to have things better in life than he had had, and learning a good trade was the way to do it.

Stoneman kept saying Sir to him. They were both about the same age, and he told Stoneman finally to stop calling him Sir. "I'm not an officer, man."

"I know you're not. It's just that anybody that did the things you did—well, you know what I mean."

"I was just working for a meat-preparing company."

"I don't exactly follow your reference. Well, anyway. My kid said he knew a boy in school named Mike Reeves, and I'd already read about you, see, so I realized we were neighbors. I try to read up on things like that. I was in service, sure, but I didn't do anything. But you guys that did fight for the country so, I figure the least I can do is read up on it."

He had encountered this before. Usually it was followed by war talk. The sooner we show Russia where to get off, the better, if you ask me. Or they'll be over here showing us. Sometimes it led into sex talk. Man might be lucky it was just his leg or eye he had to lose, you know what I mean? You take I heard about this fellow got his organ shot off. Whole genital structure, blasted right off him. Ain't that something? All right, all right, I wasn't the one. I can prove it, okay?

He was thinking of when the plane was landing. The sensation then, was like how it had been when Stoneman came to the house. Something that had returned in dreams sometimes, and would again, was that they were still waiting, did not know whether the plane would accept the runway, would last that much longer for them to find out. He was, he knew, shot bad enough, well enough, that he would not need to get into planes again for some time. Maybe not any more at all. But the being shot would be wasted, if the plane could not be landed.

It got landed. All the tires were finished. On Stoneman's car they were in good shape, but on the plane they were gashed and punctured, too much for the self-sealing to work anymore, and they were making the plane jolt and flop all the time it was moving along the concrete. Maybe that turned out to be good. The wheel mounts gave way, maybe on account of the jolting, and the plane dropped, settled, onto its belly. Because of that, it was easy to get out of, and getting the others out was easy, since it was not necessary to use the ladder. There was no firetruck or ambulance. All of them were busy already with other planes. Their plane had started burning. Several people inside it were still alive. They were not conscious, but they were alive. He got one of them out, and then another one. A radioman, Jack Benson, and the pilot, Caney Breadward, followed him back into the plane then, and they got the others out. Two of the others were dead, and the remaining ones died before long, but it was hard to tell at the time who was dead and who was not. His leg was already broken when he was doing that. He did not exactly know it, but Benson told him later that it was.

Earlier that night, the night the plane landed, he and some others had burned a city down. Which one was it. Osaka. That was the one. About a hundred planes, seven people to a plane, and the city was done for.

The debris and debris of all the slain soldiers of the war.

It was right he had come not to be bothered about the packing. They themselves were fully at rest. It was something you couldn't be taught. All you could do was learn it.

Rest easy, John. It's over now. It's over.

Mike was upstairs, in bed. Rachel was doing something up there. She was probably in Mike's room. She had done a good deal of checking, on the way back and after they were back, finding out what condition Mike was in. He was all right. He had had a good time, for the most part.

Eight years old. He himself would be twenty-seven, this year.

What was it he could do that would keep Mike from having to be in a war. There had to be something. In the war.

Déjà vu.

If he did go ahead and get well, it would have to include letting his brother leave him.

So be it.

It would mean losing a lot of good protection. The best flak jacket around.

So be it.

Study war no more.

Glenn Stoneman had got beaten, out there. His father took off his belt and held him by the collar. His grandfather said I ain't having no child whipped on my property, by his daddy or nobody. Stoneman went ahead. Rachel took Mike to the car when it started.

It had been a real beating. Glenn did not cry, or struggle. He shuddered the first few times the belt took him, but after that, nothing. No protection at all. Stoneman got finished. Then, after a minute, Stoneman said something. Not loud. "Glenn?" What happened than, Glenn drew his pistol, and pointed it at Stoneman. A cap pistol. They were in the back yard, and light was slanting across them from the porch light. Glenn was saying something to Stoneman. "I hope I'm *not* yours. I hope to hell I'm not." Stoneman became still. The look on his face, one man should not see another one look like that.

They had thought Mike would be upset about the whipping. He was calm. He had already noticed, though, that Mike didn't get upset easy.

Rachel had come downstairs.

"He wants you to come and see him. He wants you to read to him. He thinks you might be mad at him. Are you?"

"No. No, I'm not mad at him."

"He said to make it a request. If you're not too busy or anything."

"Read to me about the pig man," Mike said. "When the man came back home and nobody but the pig man knew who he was."

He found the place. "Odysseus and the Swineherd. The swineherd was sitting in front of his enclosure, round which a high wall had been built. It stood in an open space, a—"

"Daddy? Excuse me, I want to ask you something. Do people's ears fall off when they get to be twelve years old?"

"Do their ears fall off?"

"Yessir. Glenn's grandfather said they do. He said they have baby ears, and they drop off when you turn twelve."

"And then your permanent ears grow out?"

"Yessir. Do they do that?"

"No. You keep the ones you start with."

"Man. Man, am I glad to hear that. I wanted to ask you, see. Thanks a lot, you hear? Read me the rest of it now, okay?"

Rolling All the Time

Early in November, Miss Goollie told me and the others she taught the Eighth Grade to that it was time to start planning for the Thanksgiving program. The school had a program of that kind every year, and she said this year it would be a big one, with reciting and people in Pilgrim and Indian and turkey costumes. The idea came to me that if there was going to be any reciting, there could be some guitar music as well.

I could play my guitar enough by that time, since I had got it soon after school began that fall, to take a chance on being in the program with it. I had got it off my buddy Paul Vance in trade for my old man's shotgun. It took some time thinking before I made the trade. My old man had been killed the year before, and the shotgun was all that was left of anything he had owned. Once it was done, though, I realized it was the suitable step to take. By the time I had learned to do some picking, getting the guitar that way felt like coming across a chord that would let the ones that followed be the ones that were supposed to follow. We had a Health class in school, and the book told about the nerves and had illustrations of them. I could see it was a good thing they were there, with the messages flickering up and down among them, since that allowed the guitar to be played.

Paul Vance said it was a professional instrument. It had belonged to his uncle, and it had his uncle's monogram in gold letters, T.R.V., up between the frets. His uncle's name was Tucker. A week or so after he traded it, Paul got himself a new one. He paid thirteen dollars for it. That was a lot of money, and so I understood that mine had in fact cost a lot. It was big, deepest red, and after I had it waxed and shined it was glowing, and the tone it sent forth was glowing, and had purity, weight. Paul could already play, and so when Miss Goollie spoke about the Thanksgiving program I figured Paul and me could be a team.

He didn't think his parents would let him. They had been glad when he got rid of his uncle's guitar. I made out that they did not have a high regard for his uncle Tucker Vance, and before long he got around to telling me the reason. His uncle was in prison. The state prison up in Moundsville, West Virginia. I was curious why, but Paul didn't say, and since it was a family matter I didn't ask. They had not liked it when he bought himself another guitar. They were well off, and he had an allowance, but they had not intended for him to use it for that.

They went ahead and said they would not tell him not to be in the program. "Dad says I'm just rebelling against them. He says I know they'd want me to have some other interest, so I naturally chose this one."

I considered a Rebel was something good to be. If I had not been from West Virginia, my next preference would be some Rebel state, Tennessee maybe, or Georgia, or even if necessary eastern Virginia.

I had thought my aunt wouldn't want me to have a guitar either, for religious reasons. I lived with her and her family now. She surprised me, though. When I brought the guitar in, she thought it was nice. "Well of course I do, child. With the harp and the voice of a psalm, let the hills be joyful together. Psalm 98, if I recollect right." She had always been singing around the house, hymns mainly, and now sometimes when I was playing she would sing, or both of us would sing together.

On the night of the program, she was there at the school. Her husband was at home that week, my Uncle Page Cameron. He worked for the government, tending a gate at the atomic energy place over near Ohio, and usually he had to be away, but he had some days off

for the holiday. Their kids went along too. The school was down in
the town of Mt. Zion. Where we lived was up in a sort of location
called White's Gap. Mt. Zion was ten miles from us, so we loaded up
his van and he took us in.

Paul and his family—he was the only kid—lived down in the town,
but neither one of his parents came to the program. He was not
playing as well as usual. We were using western songs, and for the
end of each one we had rehearsed that the guitars would talk to each
other a minute. I would pick through something that would end
without being finished. He would answer with his guitar, and that
way the matter would be satisfied.

For the first two songs, he would not answer. I could feel the audience wanting the satisfying to take place. He was upset about his
parents not being there. Then, the third time, he did. I had to crowd
him to get him to go ahead. It involved making up some new stuff
after I had used up what we had practiced. We did the wind-up then,
and then it was over. The people applauded. They were applauding
all the contributions, and they were not going to leave us out, but it
felt good to hear them.

We had five more minutes, if we wanted them. Miss Goollie was
making motions at us from the side of the stage. She wanted to know
if we meant to stay on. I was just getting started good, and I asked
Paul in an undertone if *Columbus Stockade Blues* was okay by him.
I took his expression for yes, and I told the people we wanted to try
that one for them.

That one is an especially sad song. The man is in jail, Columbus
Stockade. Way down, not any lower to get, and everybody he trusted
in has let him down, blues. He doesn't say so, but he won't know any
better the next time either. The next chance he gets, he'll trust somebody else. After we had finished the words of it, I played without any
singing. And before long, I started crying. Not anything with any noise
to it, but something was on my face, and I realized what it was. People
could notice or not, as they liked. A man in a front row did notice, and
I heard him saying Is that kid crying? I didn't answer him except to
myself. Yeah he's crying you son of a bitch. He ain't winding his yoyo.
He said then Look at that boy swearing at me. I hadn't said a word. I

kept playing. Paul had left off when we stopped singing. I had come across a run I had not found before, and I wanted to see if it amounted to anything. The guitar was doing especially well. We had never been together as much as we were just then. Then, in a minute, I stopped playing.

Nobody applauded this time. They had not liked *Columbus Stockade Blues*. Tough on them. It was mainly myself I was playing for anyway.

The man in the front row did applaud a little, then. A few more did.

Then, a lot of people were. Everybody in the place was, and they kept on. Miss Goollie had come out onto the stage with us, and when they were getting quiet she was saying Encore? If we ask them nicely, these young gentlemen might give us an encore.

But I was done. I got myself unstrapped from the guitar, and left. There was something I wanted. I didn't know what it was. I was jumpy about something. Maybe it would go away by itself.

I hadn't told the people So long or Thanks or anything at all. The next contribution was already started, and I couldn't go back and tell them.

Then I couldn't anyway. I had to get out in the air. I sat on the back steps and bent over, and that way kept from getting any sicker. The schoolyard looked strange. This was the first time I had seen it at night, but still it was just the schoolyard. It looked like I had been away somewhere and forgot about it.

The town of Mt. Zion had an Oddfellows Hall, and Miss Goollie mentioned one day that the Oddfellows were having a program themselves, connected with Christmas. The man that thought I was swearing at him was a friend of hers. His name was Beacham, and he was with the Oddfellows. She said that if we wanted to, Vance and me could be in that program.

Paul's parents refused again to tell him no, so he went ahead. My uncle was away at work this time, and Miss Goollie arranged a ride for me down to Mt. Zion. I was going to walk, but she objected until we agreed she would come up to where we met the school bus. Her friend Mr. Beacham used his car. She said to sit up front with them, but I got in the back seat, to have room to take care of the guitar. They talked about how isolated the country up in here was. I didn't know what we were isolated from, unless it was Mt. Zion, and that was not a disadvantage. She was telling him our young friend has the most astonishing contact with the audience, and he said my word yes, he had felt it himself.

The Oddfellows Hall had a room where people in the program could wait until their turn came. We were early, and I was the only one in there at first. I tuned my guitar. I had to tune it whenever I brought it down from White's Gap, because of the change in altitude. The neck of it had some dents on the underside, up near the end. It looked like something had been gnawing on it. That part of the neck also had some dark stains. I knew what they came from, because I had made some of them. They were sweat stains, from the left hand. There was also a faint hollow worn into the wood up there, from the heel of the left hand being moved in that neighborhood. It would take many an hour and many an hour of playing, to get a wear-mark like that one. Sometimes I shined the monogram, the gold initials. It didn't get dull, because it was genuine gold, but I shined it anyway. I waxed the wood sometimes. I knew now that the guitar had not been in best condition when I got it. Nobody had been using it. Such instruments need to be used. Often I had the feeling that this one wanted to be used. Sometimes after I had played something that worked out all right, I had the feeling that it was willing for me to be the user. A while back I had had a notion to send a card or letter or something to T.R.V. Paul said what do you want to send a card to *him* for. I didn't know, and I didn't know what I would say in one, so I never sent one.

With Paul and me, things went better that night than they had at the school. We did three western songs, and three railroad songs. He asked me not to do *Columbus Stockade* again, or any prison song. When I thought the other night he had been giving me an okay about it, he had been saying No. This time, at the end of the playing, I remembered to tell the people we appreciated getting to play for them. Before I could say it, though, Mr. Beacham was there. He asked the people to give us a big hand, and they did, and he told our names again. Then we shook hands, and him and Paul shook hands. And that was it. Or I thought so, but there was one more thing.

He paid me ten dollars for the playing. He did it privately, and asked me to sign a receipt. I thought at first it was his personal money and I would need to decline it, but it was from the ticket proceeds. The school program had been free, but here people had paid to get in. It came to me that since he was paying me privately, Vance was not getting paid. Paul's parents were well off, and whatever me and Kenna and her family were, it was not well off. But that was okay by me. "The laborer is worthy of his hire. Scripture." That was what she said sometimes. I had not labored, and it was a joy and a pleasure to me to be playing, but being paid was still fair dealing.

Now that I had some money I could pay him for bringing me down here. He looked sort of funny when I asked him how much it was worth to him. Then he said the travel was included as part of the payment. Down here, and back as well. "We're even, Tyler. Okay? Why don't you go on out front now, and watch the rest of the entertainment?"

I stayed in the waiting room. Paul had already left. I had a comic with me, *Gunn Belt*, and I read in it. Once I took out the ten dollar bill. The picture on it showed Alexander Hamilton. He looked like a town person. He looked like somebody that wouldn't want to know places like White's Gap, or West Virginia, or people that were not well off, existed. That was okay. With ten bucks I wasn't going to worry about the expression on the face of the picture.

I could buy the guitar some new strings tomorrow. Tonight, the stores were closed already. It hardly ever broke any, but now I could get a complete set of spares. Blazing Ruby. I had used Crystal Chimes, and Pretty Pickings, but Blazing Ruby was the best kind I had come across.

The last week before Christmas, the American Legion in Bridgeport had a program. Bridgeport was sixty miles away, up towards Wheeling. Mr. Beacham had talked to the people there, and Paul and me could be in it. For that one, Paul's parents would not give him permission. It was too far away, and they wanted him to study for the exams that were coming. The arrangement that got made was that I would be in the Legion program by myself.

It would be on a Friday, and I stayed out of school that week to practice. Aunt Kenna wanted me to include a religious song among the four I would do. She suggested *Walking in Sunlight*. The two of us had several times sung and played that one.

"I just wish it could be sunlight for you all the time, child. I don't reckon you'll be staying around here long, though."

"Aunt Kenna, I'm not going nowhere."

At the Legion Hall in Bridgeport, I saw as soon as I went in that I had got into more than I knew anything about. The other times, Paul and I were doing the only guitar playing. At school, somebody had done card tricks, and he had dropped his cards. A lady at the Oddfellows was giving Lincoln's Gettysburg Address, and when she forgot part of it she just explained she had forgot and went to the part she remembered. At the Legion, it was not a program at all. It was a regular show.

A band, the Four Ridge Runners, professionals, were going to have all the last ninety minutes of it. Only three of them were in the waiting room when I got there, but they had a red and yellow Pontiac in the parking lot with the name of their outfit on it, and guitars and a fiddle and banjos and a dulcimer and a mandolin in the waiting room, along with microphones and electrical equipment. They were talking about whether to use their own equipment, or what the Hall had. I was going to be the third one to do anything, in the show. Four girls, the Kissing Cousins, were going to be on for fifteen minutes, and after them a man and a woman were going to waltz and do other dances.

The three men in the Ridge Runners were looking me over. I heard one of them say What are we doing in the same show with a kid? Another one answered him We're making some coins if I'm not mistaken. And then, they were looking at me some more. This time, it was the guitar.

The one that had been talking most came over, and he was about to pick it up. I had seen what he had on his mind, and I had moved between him and the table I had put it on. "Where'd you get that guitar, fellow?"

It was the one that had wanted to know what they were doing in a show with a kid. I hadn't liked his looks anyway, and they were not improving. One of the others said Take it easy, Fuller. Fuller kept talking. "You Tucker Vance's boy?" One of the others told him Tucker didn't have no kids. "Come on back over here, Fuller. What do you want to pester that boy for?" Fuller went back over. They were talking some more "He does act a little like Tucker, though. You remember old Tucker wouldn't let anybody mess with it?" And some more, and then they were back to talking about whose equipment to use. After a time, Beacham and another man looked in. Beacham said Come on. I was going to be the next one to go on.

I had expected to be nervous about having to be out there by myself. I didn't seem to mind. The manager lowered the microphone, and said to sing straight into it. Hearing myself and the guitar being amplified was a shock, but not a bad one. Things went maybe better than when Paul and me played as a team. People here clapped in a polite way. At the Oddfellows they had made more noise about it. The men here were wearing suits and neckties, and the women were dressed up. I had a thought of seeing if I could make them clap a lot anyway. Then I figured that would be fighting them. Even so, by the third song they were loosened up a little. I had picked out a girl in a row near the front. She was older than me. Then I picked out another one. The last song, though, was *Walking In Sunlight,* and it seemed better to leave them alone. Not that they knew I had been doing anything with them.

I had been nervous after all. I had the beginning of a belly cramp, and I wanted a lot of something that would be cold. Ice water maybe. It was a little like the night at school. I wanted to avoid seeing those guys in the waiting room again. I wished they would clear out so I could have it to myself.

Another one was with them by then. He made the fourth. He was younger than they were. He was thin.

He came over to me. "Howdy."

"How you doing."

"You the one that's got Tucker Vance's guitar?"

"I got my own guitar."

He wanted to see it. To examine it. Then I decided he didn't look like he would be any more of a bastard that he could help being. The others were sort of laughing. "Smith, we told you to keep clear of that kid. He stopped Fuller in his tracks." I held the guitar out to him. He took it. He turned it various ways. The monogram was easy to notice. "That's Tucker's all right. That's his. It sounded like his the minute I walked in the building." He also located the dents on the underside of the neck. "Coon did that. It was trying to get some salt. Your hand gets sweaty, and salt gets in the wood." He looked at me. "How'd you get this?" He had handled the guitar in a proper way, so I was willing to tell him. But this was not the time and place, so I only told him I'd got it off a fellow. He nodded. "We thought it was lost." He looked over at the others. "He had it that last night. You know? Blood all over him, that night." I told him he could play on it if he wanted to. When he went ahead, I wished I hadn't said he could. I had considered myself able to play. I had stood up and showed my face to people on the basis of considering myself able to. His fingers dwelt on the strings, and there was a spray, a flowering, for a minute. And it ceased. By that time, I was glad I had told him he could go ahead. Not many times happened that you got to hear music that had that much truth to it.

"That's Tucker's, all right," he said.

He put out a hand, and we shook hands. "My name's Stonefield Smith. I live over near Romney."

So I told him my name, and where I lived. He had heard of the place. I knew where Romney was from looking on road maps. And up in that section there was a creek that had ice on it even in hot weather. From the way he had played, and from his face as well, it did not feel surprising that he came from a section where something like that could occur.

He was young. Older than me by several years, but still young.

"Tucker ain't home, is he? Or do you know?"

I told him as far as I knew he was not.

"Didn't think I'd heard anything about him being back." He handed the guitar back to me. "Thanks a lot, okay? You did pretty good with this thing out there. Enjoyed hearing you."

I said something in return.

"You okay, partner?"

I still had the belly cramp.

"Sure you are. It gets you a little, don't it, when you first come off?"

He smiled. He said he got to do some ridge running pretty soon. We shook hands again, and he went back over to the others.

He was telling them they would use the hall's mikes and amps. One of them, Fuller, began to argue, but Stonefield Smith said they would use the hall's

For being in programs, that was it. Christmas ended, and matters were back to routine. I had made twenty dollars in all. I got another set of guitar strings so as to be secure. Aunt Kenna was usually able to keep back fifteen cents for me to get a new one when necessary, but now I had a supply.

I also got some stick-on letters, for my initials, Tyler Glasgow Ansted. I had played in public now, not just in a school program, and I had in mind to put them on my guitar. The T.R.V. letters, the gold ones, had screws to hold them in. Very small screws, and I was using the point of my jackknife to take them out. While I was trying to get the first one started, though, the jackknife closed on my hand. The whetted edge, just behind the nails of my right hand. That was the picking hand. There was a considerable amount of blood. Some got on the guitar. I wiped it off the guitar with my other hand, and after a time the cuts had stopped bleeding. They were not deep, but I figured I might as well let things stay as they were.

Aunt Kenna accepted five dollars to get some Christmas stuff, and I kept five dollars for reserve. I meant for it to be reserve. I broke it to buy a chording manual one day, and the rest of it melted away.

Late that winter, in March, a man I had not seen before showed up at Paul's house. He was quiet. He was not young, but he looked like he ought to be young. It was his eyes that made him look that way. He was old enough to be getting puffy, but there was none of that whatever. In the face, he was weathered. This was Paul's uncle that had been in prison. We didn't get introduced, but I realized anyway that this was Tucker Vance. Maybe it was the family resemblance that told me who he was. What I really thought, though, I knew him from using his guitar.

If I had seen him before, I'd never have touched it. Now that I had, I felt like I had got away with something.

It had not been Paul's to trade.

Paul wanted me to go in another room with him. "I want to tell you something. Whatever we do, I mean if we play anything, don't make it *Columbus Stockade.* Where he can hear us, okay? My point is, he might not know how to take it. Since he's been in—you know—himself, see. Prison."

From the glimpse I had had of Tucker Vance I figured there was little he would not know how to take.

"He was in for killing. I had to tell you about it, see. So you'd know nothing's the matter in case he starts acting peculiar. You can't ever tell what one of these—convicts— is going to do."

Paul's parents did not want him to play a guitar or be in the programs because that was what his uncle used to do. Tucker had made his living as a guitar player. When I remembered how the men in the Bridgeport Hall had said his name, I knew there could not be a better one. Paul's father was embarrassed, and Mrs. Vance was embarrassed and alarmed, about having him in their house, about being related to him. I never heard either of them, or Paul, speak to him by his name. She did not have Paul, or me, stay in his vicinity more than a minute or so at a time. When she talked to him she was extremely polite, so as to be unfriendly. Tucker had not made much of a living at any time. Paul said his father had remarked how Tucker had always insisted on doing things his own way.

Tucker Vance was through with music now. He was at Paul's house to try and get a job in Mt. Zion. His hopes were to work for his brother, Paul's father. Mr. Vance, Jabal Vance, owned houses, and he was part owner of an automobile agency, and partners in three or four other things. Paul's house had deep rugs and heavy furniture, and a patio and terrace instead of a yard. His mother had said once, "I'm very happy you and Paul are friends, Tyler. I've been anxious for him to meet a wide range of people." Jobs were hard to get, in Mt. Zion or anywhere. I had often heard Kenna say what a providence it was that her husband had permanent work. For anybody with a prison record, they were impossible. Tucker was going to be a janitor in his brother Jabal's car agency.

Kenna had heard of Tucker Vance. I mentioned to her that he was staying at Paul's house. From her and Paul together, I got the picture of what had happened. The one he had killed was a man that took up with his wife. The man's name was Pommie Packer. I already knew about the Packers. They lived around Skater's Creek, over in Virginia. I had heard things about Skater's Creek, and the feeling was that nobody decent would live there longer than they could help. The thing Kenna could not understand was why Tucker's wife had got mixed up with anybody from the Packer family at all. Tucker went to the motel where the two of them had gone. He had been playing at a dance that night. One thing led to the next, and eventually Tucker had carved him with his Barlow knife. He did not have the knife out when things started. There was a chance his wife was going to go on back with him. When Pommie Packer saw it might be that way, Pommie slapped her to one side. Tucker moved in on him then. Pommie far outweighed him, and outreached him, and after a time Tucker was fighting for his life. It looked that way, and it was possible in the trial he could have got clear, or almost clear. When they asked him though why he had done it, he said the furrow had been started and he was going to plow to the end of it. "Did you intend to take his life?" "Judge, sir, I meant to see the bastard fall." And when he said that, his friends gave a groan. He got five years in state prison. His time was finished early in February, and now here he was.

His wife was long gone. She came from Mobile, Alabama, or one of those places. He had met her down there when he had been making some trips as a tanker seaman. She got a divorce while he was in prison, and maybe she had gone back down there.

"They ought to sent one of them Packers to jail instead of him," Kenna said. "Have one less around here. That judge ought to thanked Mr. Vance for doing away with that one."

I regretted he was finished with music. It could have come about that he would teach me some things. If he had told me anything I would have done it over and over until it got an okay. With him telling me, I could have got it right almost the first time. He was working every day now, Paul said, except Sundays, sweeping floors and cleaning the toilets in the car agency. And so I knew now what it meant about a prophet without honor among his own.

I had it in mind not to go to Paul's house anymore. In the near future I would need to be somewhere else altogether. I had heard that fellow named Stonehill, or Stonefield, in Bridgeport, and I knew that what I could do here was close to nothing. I did not know where to turn. But what I needed was not here.

I was at Paul's house, on the patio, one afternoon. I would not be visiting there anymore. He could meet a wide range of people without me being included. I had invited him twice to visit at the Cameron house, but he had not been able to. Mrs. Vance had asked me if my aunt did any crafts, such as quilting or weaving. "I understand many of our residents keep up the old crafts. I'd love to meet your aunt." I had gone by this time to get my chording manual. Easter vacation was starting, and I would just discontinue visiting there.

Paul wanted to do some picking. He was playing back-up. We did something or other, and then he stopped and I was playing on my own. It was *New River Train*. No singing. Just the playing. In a minute, his uncle had come to the door that opened onto the patio. His uncle stood there listening.

I didn't know if Paul had told him about me having the guitar. When he saw me using it, of course he knew I had it. He was not concerned with those things anymore, though.

Paul's mother was at an upstairs window. "Paul dear. Would you come here a moment? We have got to have an understanding about things."

"I got to go," Paul said. "Boy, she's mad. I told her I wouldn't play anymore."

I was glad I had already decided to discontinue visiting. She was probably going to discontinue it for me. Earlier that afternoon she had been talking to me in an extremely polite way. I kept on playing. Tucker was listening. I brought it to an end, and went over to him, with the guitar.

"Mr. Tucker, this is yours."

He watched me for a while. "It's yours, son. I don't know how you got it, but you got it honest."

"Will you teach me how to play it?"

He watched me some more. "Son, where are you from?"

"White's Gap."

"Who are you kin to up there?"

"The Camerons." He was asking me my name. He thought enough of himself not to ask it point-blank. "My name's Tyler Ansted, Mr. Tucker.".

"What makes you think I can teach you anything, son?"

He had a kind of smile. It went away. It was not me he was smiling at. Life and the world, maybe, but he was not actually amused even at them. I recalled how he had gone to where his wife and the other man were and battled with him and killed him. The men in Bridgeport had spoken of him. He had also been in ships on the ocean. Five years behind bars were also in that smile.

"What makes you think I can teach you anything?"

He was watching me. We were watching each other.

By summertime, I was going along with Tucker to performances. He had decided to go back to playing. He had swept floors for ten days at the agency, and on the Friday he got his pay, forty-eight dollars, he told his brother he was resigning his position. He got himself a forty-dollar guitar and a three-dollar-and-fifty-cent bottle of applejack, and restrung his guitar with a set of Blazing Rubies and filled in with a band that was playing that same night in a place on the road to Charleston. They had had time to get the word around that he was going to be there, and people came in numbers and from distances, and he made them to lie down in green pastures. The novelty was over after the first few times and they were back in their backsliding ways, but he was still getting enough playing jobs to keep him going. All the off time he had, we practiced. In June, soon after school was out, was when I first went along with him.

Kenna was willing to have it. She had been glad to make Tucker's acquaintance. Some of the places we went to were honkytonks, and although she could not approve of them she accepted Tucker's word that they were not lowdown. He was not misleading her. Most of them closed by midnight, and nearly all the customers were just ordinary people and their wives or girlfriends. The lowdown places had jukeboxes anyway, or nothing, instead of live entertainment.

The two of us together began getting more work than he was getting by himself. Places would book a team sooner than they would one man. It was an asset also for me to be as young as I was. I was fifteen that year, and people came to see us partly because we were that murder convict and that kid. They stayed, and they came back, because we didn't let them down as to the music. And also, I had started singing, and singing was something people expected with the playing. Aunt Kenna was not surprised we were getting plenty of work. "It's the time of year for it, child. The gifts of the Holy Spirit come down, about this time of year."

I was able to pay her for my board and room, and get myself some clothes. She said I didn't need to pay anything, but I started putting in ten dollars a week. In addition we got ourselves a station wagon, a four-year-old Chevy. He had been using a pick-up truck he had bought back in the spring for thirty dollars. It didn't travel exactly the direction the position of the steering wheel would lead you to think it was going to, and it sort of trembled when it was in motion. The Chevy was good transportation. It was a light blue color, easy-handling, and it would move out when we were short of time and wanted it to or when I wanted it to—I could make it go vroom—and he didn't say slow down.

One day when he drove up on the mountain to the Cameron house, he wanted me to look at something. The front doors of the station wagon had signs painted on them. *Tuck & Ti*. And underneath, *Country & Bluegrass*. All of it in silver letters. Kenna was impressed. "Well ain't that the prettiest thing." I was impressed myself. The lettering was professional, and it was flowing and silver and clean. One of her kids was starting to tell him my name was not spelt with an *i,* but she told it to be quiet. Tucker wanted to know if I thought the signs looked okay.

"Sure, Tuck. They're fine, sure.—How come you put your name first, though?" I moved out of reach before he could punch me.

He was not going to. "Tell him, Miss Kenna. Tell Mr. Ansted who's in charge of this group."

I decided not to go back to school that fall. I didn't know what she would say about it, but she said it was all right if I thought it was suitable. What did bother her was I decided to move away. It would be to Annistown, a medium-size place over in Virginia. It was only a hundred miles, but it was the moving away at all that she gave thought to. She said though that she had foreseen it would happen. I remembered she had once said as much.

Tucker and I had been making many trips into Virginia during the last part of the summer. We had been playing mostly in places on that side of the state line. I used to go over there two or three times a month, when my old man would take pulpwood logs to the papermill in the town of Covington, Virginia. When we had sold a load of logs we not only had some money again, and he said it was we because I was swinging an axe with him and helping load and drive the truck, and he would be feeling good with liquor he would buy with a little of the money, but we could recross the state line and be back in West Virginia. After he got killed, in a rockslide one morning, I used to hang around our cabin a lot, and sometimes sleep out in the woods. Eventually I stopped with that, and I gained some weight back. My old lady died when I was too young to remember her. I told Tucker about some of that time. He didn't say anything. But when he got up, he put his hand down on my shoulder. And that was all he did.

The places Tucker and I were playing in were hard to get to from White's Gap. The part of the country where we were getting work was in a valley, Shenandoah country, with more towns and people, customers, than back in here. If we lived over there we would not need to keep crossing the mountains, cutting into our practice time and putting wear on the car. I had also decided that when we got over there I wanted a place of my own to live in. I was studying how I would let him know, since I didn't want him to think I didn't want his company. It turned out that he had the same idea. He also wanted a place of his own.

She cooked a big dinner when we were leaving. He had a present for her and the house. It was a set of eight table glasses. When you flicked the rims they would ping. Three of them had good F-sharps. The others just gave pings. I had a new cloth for the table. For him, and me, she had made flannel shirts, gray ones. She had got the measurements for his from one he had left laying around. And on mine, she had put two outsize pockets and on each pocket she had made a Rebel flag. The diagonals, and the thirteen stars. It was a pleasure being related to somebody like her. Much fine stitching in the flags. You could hardly make out the stitching.

Tucker put his on while he was there. When he did, I saw some marks across his back. I had not been in the room before when he changed shirts. When I asked him what the marks were, he said he had got them up at the place. In a minute, I figured out he meant the prison. They had whipped him up there. He was saying then, Take it easy, Ty. I went on outside. I thought about kicking a tree down, or beating some down with my hands or butting them down with my head. Gunn Belt could have snapped them without any effort. I kept working to get enough air to breathe. Finally I did get enough, and enough again.

I noticed a rock close by. Limestone. A long flat one, three feet thick, more than three. Something had made it flat, and made scratches on it. The glacier had been here once. Deep scratches. But the ice was gone now, and the rock was still here.

Afterwhile I went on back to the house.

When we were leaving, she said I could still change my mind if I wanted to, and I would always have a place to come to as long as she had one. "Tucker Vance, you better take good care of him. If you don't, the Lord Jesus will make you pay for it forever. I know you were sent through the valley of the shadow and brought back, but that ain't nothing to what will happen if you let any harm come to him."

Sometimes in the honkytonks I saw men I had seen before, in Paul's house or in the auditoriums before Christmas. Back then, I took them to be respectable substantial people. They were. They had late model cars or new ones, and they wore clothes that had to cost a good deal, and some of them used the kind of voices that educated people have. In the honkytonks, however, they were with women Tucker had spoken to me about. He knew I was horny, and he pointed out that I probably already knew that some women were going women. They might not want to bother with anybody my age, but then again. There were others besides them, though, and it would be using sense to leave the others alone. It was always the others that the well-dressed men were with. The men were out getting themselves a little. They were cutting loose for the night. They were tearing up the pea-patch. It was depressing. Those women were their choice. Being with them was part of cutting loose. The honkytonk owners didn't always let those women in, with or without their tricks. The men would tell the owner Do you know who I am, Do you think I can't buy and sell you, but the manager had heard it before.

One night Jabal Vance himself was in a place where we were playing. The times I had seen him before, he had been chilly and giving orders. Tonight, he was unsteady on his legs, and extra-jolly. If I had been Tucker, that would have been all the repayment I needed for having to hear Mrs. Vance be over-polite, for sweeping floors and cleaning commodes in the car agency. Or maybe there could not have been enough repayment. Most likely, Tucker was not interested. Jabal Vance wanted to shake hands with us and introduce us to the woman he had with him. Tucker already knew her name, and he told me to go bring him his new guitar pick. I didn't know he had a new one, and then I saw he wanted me to clear out. The next day he said he guessed I knew people had different sides to them. He was not going to apologize for his kin, but I thought he might be referring to Jabal Vance.

I could meet girls about my age, since Tucker knew people that had teen-age daughters or relatives. One of his friends was Stone-field Smith, that I had met in Bridgeport once. More than a year ago now. The band Smith had back then was out of business now. Smith had a job, that he hated the guts of, but he filled in whenever he could with other bands. Sometimes he joined in with us. I had heard him on the guitar, but he was mainly a fiddle man. He could sing okay, and now and then when Smith and I were singing together, we played around with it. He could bay like a hound, and squeak, and make clicking sounds, and sometimes if a song had to do with how mean somebody's woman had treated him and how depressed he felt about it, Smith would bay. He had a cousin, a year older than me. She was pretty, but she was in school and her friends were, and they were concerned with teams and grades and similar matters. For me to be making my living by the means I had, to be working at all, made being around them odd.

The girls I myself wanted to meet were older than me by more than a year or two. After I met some of them, I thought they might become either going women or tramps after they themselves got older. For the time being, they were neither. The station wagon turned out to be the kind of vehicle to have. You could stretch out in it. This was springtime again, but late at night, the free time I usually had, it still got cold, and I kept a couple of blankets in the back. There was something perfect about going to sleep afterwards wrapped up in the blankets with whoever it was.

My father had told me the facts of life, but I had not been around other fellows enough to get further information. Tucker didn't do much talking about it. I was singing one night, and for some reason he looked at me. My voice had become deeper lately, and it was getting a rasp. He listened a while. A day or so later he gave me a flat tin box. "You know what these are, I guess." I sort of did, so I said Sure. He smiled. "What are they, then? Okay. Don't actually have to use them. They're city stuff. Suit yourself. They got this kind here. Kind named Sheik. Monarchs. Semper Fidelis." It reminded me of the names of guitar strings. He also had a little tube of ointment. "Here. Axle grease."

Sex and guitar playing had some connection with each other. That is, they had connection to the same thing. I remembered the illustrations of the nerves. I had thought back then how dark and hot and wet it must be back inside where the nerves lived. I would think also sometimes, now, find out, how it could be icy silent as well, glowing at times, at times howling. Once in a while when things went especially well and kept going for a good while, I could assemble new runs on the strings, that had never been found before. Some of them I could locate again later, and get memorized, and whenever I played them, people in the audience would pay attention. They enjoyed it, and that was good, but I think Tucker knew where they came from. Rather, how I had got to them. He had not lived thirty-eight years for nothing. Nobody really knew, eye hath not seen nor ear heard, where such things come from. But the music was a way to remind people they were there, a way to ask for them. To get to even one, you would be willing to live thirty-eight years for nothing, and thirty-eight times thirty-eight.

In the fall, I found another place to live. It was still in Annistown, but it had advantages. The first place was a residence with rooms to rent, and the she-bear that ran it kept track to the minute of when I left and when I came back. I moved to a place that was a combination hotel and rooming house. It was in a lowclass part of town, but the people that lived there looked all right. They just didn't have much money. I could have company there, a girl, provided we were careful. There was no slipping around. We just didn't do any advertising.

Tucker had a girl of his own for a time, and later another one. They were towards his age. I didn't get to know them beyond passing the time of day. He had a strong feeling of privacy about things.

Three men in the Packer family, always the same three, sometimes came to the places we would be playing in. They were brothers of Pommie Packer, the one Tucker had knifed. Sometimes a state trooper would come in soon after them. The Packers were known about on both sides of the state line, and whenever the troopers did not have anything else to do they would find some Packers to follow. The three brothers I saw were good-looking in a sticky way.

Managers at most of the places would get them out as soon as they came in, if they got in. They only came for Tucker to know they were there. I was not able sometimes to tell if he had noticed them.

The three of them overtook us late one afternoon, when we were going from Annistown to the place we would be playing in that night. I was the one driving at the time, and Tucker said to stay put. He meant not to go any faster or slower. They tailgated us for eleven miles. It was Stevie Packer driving their car. In the side mirror, our looks met a couple of times, mine and Stevie's, but his expression stayed the same. Eventually, he turned their car up a sideroad.

Tucker did not carry a weapon at all anymore, a pocket knife or any kind. He owned a .45 Smith & Wesson, and after the tailgating, I took it, without letting him know, when we were practicing in his room once. I put it in the Chevy dash compartment. He found it and put it back in his room.

"You leave it there, Ansted. You hear me?"

"Yessir."

I was interested that he was not afraid of the Packers. I was not afraid of them myself, but it was not me they were busying themselves about. "I might be afraid of the Holy Ghost, Tyler, or like that. I hope I am anyway. Them Packers don't bother me none."

One place we played in, I especially liked. It was the farthest from where we lived, over a hundred miles to the south, below Bluefield and west. What I liked about it was that some of the customers would dance in a way different from the usual dancing we saw. The ones who did that were the older people. Couples could join in, but usually it would only be old men dancing. Down there, women by that age were too worn out to be dancing anymore. It was clog-dancing. The young people didn't go for it, so it was mostly just those old men. You needed to keep yourself loose, and let your arms hang free, and bring your shoes down solid. You could stomp on somebody's foot or get your own stomped, if you didn't know what you were doing. The patterns were not simple.

The first night we were there, and the times afterwards, I went out onto the floor and clogged with them. I wore boots for it. Clog-dancing needed to be done with heavy shoes. Sometimes we would have the building shuddering with the beat we were into. The building had a wooden floor, broad-boards, oak boards cut broad the way they were cut in the old days, and we could get a pretty good shudder going. I would go back up on the platform before long, so as to stay with the music, his guitar and mine talking to each other, his giving mine the beat and mine giving it back, and Jesus, man. I like to work. I'm rolling all the time. Those old guys would buy me Nehis afterwards. They figured I was too young for hard liquor.

I was getting on towards eighteen by then, and I had found out that I liked liquor. The first time I played in public, that long time ago at school one night, I had wanted something afterwards. It was liquor, although I didn't know at the time. A good many times now I wanted some, when things were through for the night. Tucker now and then had some. It would usually be applejack. I asked him for some of it one night after we had finished and me and him and the manager and the two waitresses were sitting around before we started home. He waited, but then he went ahead and poured some into a glass. "If you're old enough to work for it, I reckon you're old enough to drink it." I wished it had occurred to me sooner. Once he had whiskey, Old Forester, and I liked that better. "Most people do, Tyler. Most people do." I gathered it was expensive. Tucker would do the actual buying. Once he said he had just as soon not get any. "You don't realize how much you're drinking, do you?"

"I got to have some way to unwind, Tucker."

"That ain't what I said. This is going to be the third one this week. Why not just leave it at two?" So we did. It was only pints, but we still did.

It was not all the time that we could afford such extras. The summer of that year, things were the way he had said they sometimes were. The Republicans had got in, and they had been in long enough to get a recession going, and a number of places had quit using live entertainment, or closed up entirely. We got all but broke. We had pawned my record player. It was a quality high fidelity outfit. He said that if a performer was good enough to listen to at all, a quality player was the kind to get. When that money gave out and we still had not got work, he pawned one of his guitars, the forty-dollar one he had bought when he went back to playing. He had another one now that he had paid two hundred for. With the money from that, we put gas in the station wagon and drove to the city of Roanoke.

In Roanoke there was a spot-labor office run by the GladHands Company. Tucker had worked out of one of their places in Pittsburgh the first week he was out of prison. People could hire through them by the day, and load trucks or move stock in warehouses or do other manual labor. The GladHands office opened at five-thirty a.m. We were there at five, and people were already waiting for it to open.

Some of the people there didn't get work that morning. Tucker and I were lucky, and both of us did. We worked alongside each other off-loading trailer trucks of canned goods onto a conveyor track at a wholesale place. Other days, sometimes we both got work at the same place, sometimes we had to split up. The pay was ninety cents an hour. At five p.m. we reported back to the office and got our money. You got paid the same day you worked. We did that for two weeks, and that was how we managed. We did not get jobs every day of those two weeks. The first one, I got six days and he got four. The second one, I got four and he got two. The days he did not get out, he checked on bookings for us. He would be at GladHands when people got through, and we would go back to Annistown.

One afternoon when we were headed back, we had stopped at a hamburger place for supper. In the booth, he was writing something. I figured it was words for a song. Now and then we did write them. I had got two or three that we used, and we used several of his. He knew how to notate music, and read it. Not so many guitar pickers did. He stopped for a minute. "Therefour. Is it t-h-e-i-r, or t-h-i-e-r?" I told him t-h-e-r-e. "Thanks." He had had to quit school and go to work when he finished the fifth grade. His brother, three years younger than him, had been able to keep going. "What about the rest of it? F-o-r-e, right?"

"Right."

He considered me. "Look, Tyler. You don't have to worry about making me feel bad. I know I don't know much. How do you spell it?"

So I told him the right way. "F-o-u-r, Tuck." He was satisfied then. I wanted to see the song when he was finished, but he said it was not ready yet.

That night, he had a telephone call at his place. I was there already, since we were practicing. There was a pay phone in the front hall, and when he came back he had got us a booking. Stonefield Smith had been working on it too, and the three of us were lined up for tomorrow, which was Friday, and for Saturday as well, both nights at the Colonial Manor Supper Club.

The three of us had played there once before. The last several months, Stoney had been with us on a good many jobs. Tucker had asked me how I felt about changing the signs on the station wagon, and they read now, *Stonefield, Tuck & Ti.* Smith was about the only one that had visited him from time to time in the prison, and kept in touch with him. The Colonial Manor was a pretty big place, out from Bluefield, and we had fine crowds both nights. We had to play for a percentage instead of a straight fee, but what with the crowds, and the special requests when somebody would send up a dollar or two bucks or several times a bug-eye five to hear a particular song, we had a jackpot. And we were in the money again.

Saturday night after we had finished I asked him to get some Old Forester for me. He agreed on condition that if any driving was done he would do it. But I could drive almost any time, and Old Forester was not always around.

The next afternoon, he came in, for practice. I was not having any part of practice. He said we would practice, so we started. I had some scratches on my face. Once or twice I had been punching with somebody, when a girl was in process of going along with me instead of them, but there had not been any of that last night. After a time I put the guitar down and went into the bathroom. Eventually he called through the door. "If you're done puking, Ansted, we can get back to work." Sometimes when he called me Ansted, it was like he hardly knew me. We got the practicing done. We had missed very few days at practicing and rehearsing. He was somebody to count on.

"Tyler?"

"Yessir?"

"You know these fellows we see sometimes? You said something once like they were tearing up the pea-patch?"

I knew what was coming next.

"That's what you were doing last night, Tyler."

Finally, I said something. "Why didn't you stop me, Tuck?"

"I don't actually know. I've been thinking about it. Maybe it's times when a man has to stop himself."

Afterwhile he said something else. "Listen. Don't look like that, Tyler. It's not any disaster."

"I won't do that no more, Tuck."

"It's no disaster. Look here. I tell you what."

He left for a minute. When he came back, he had a banjo. When I saw it, I had some sort of recollection from last night that had him and a banjo and somebody at a filling station in it. I had been on top of the station wagon, clogging, and he was saying All right, come on down from there. I told him and the filling station man they would have to come up after me. They didn't pay any attention, and when I was coming down, I slipped on the gravel and that was how my face got the scratches. The filling station man gave me a hand getting up. I thought for a minute I had hurt my picking hand, but it was all right. Tucker checked it out too. I had managed to take the fall on my left hand. Or not even that. The forearm. The filling station man said he certainly did like hearing us play. I offered to play a little old number for him right then, and Tucker said Get in the car. Just get in the car. The banjo was handmade. He was giving it to me. The drumhead was groundhog hide, the best material around for banjo heads.

He had something else. He took it out of his pocket, a small leather case. "Tyler, don't you think you might like to put your initials on your guitar sometime?" That was what he had in the case. Gold ones, with screws to fasten them on. T, and G, and A.

It would mean taking his off. And I was not in favor of that. I took the ones he was giving me, but I wanted his to stay on. "If it's all right with you, Tuck. You don't mind, do you?"

He didn't answer for a minute. "I don't mind, Ansted. I'm glad that's the way you want it."

When he called me Ansted this time it was like he knew me good.

He had noticed the jackknife scars, but I had held off from telling him how they had got there. I figured I would sometime, sooner or later.

Early one afternoon, a car horn was sounding in front of where I lived. I had been asleep, and when I started hearing it there was the feeling it had been going on for some time. Tucker had told once about the foghorns on ships when they were calling danger. A girl named Naomi was with me. Had been. She had woke up and left already. I wished the noise would stop. After a time, I recognized it. When I looked, the Chevy was stopped in the street. Not parked by the curb, and Tucker was slumped down over the steering wheel. I got my shoes on, and my shirt and pants on getting down the stairs. It seemed like I already knew what had happened. Like I already knew it from long back.

I had to shove him over so as to get behind the wheel. I looked at him for long enough to let him know that I was going to do it. I was going to anyway, but it was fitting to get an okay from him. He looked back, so I knew he realized it was necessary. I held him up while I did so he would not fall over. I knew it was hurting. He moaned, and the urine let go in his trousers from the pain. They had drove him down as low as they could, and now I was having to bring him lower still. There was not much blood, coming out. I could see the bullet hole, up above his belt buckle. There was a patch of blood around it, crusty already. A hemorrhage inside would be as bad. Worse.

The hospital was three miles out of town, on the other side of town. On the way, he wanted me to stop and play to him. Both the guitars were already in the back. I thought at first he was out of his head, but he meant it. I told him there was not time. He still wanted me to stop the car, and play something.

"Don't you do requests on your show, Tyler?"

"You're hurt, Tuck. We've got to get you to the hospital."

"It don't hurt except when you go pushing on me."

"I had to do that, Tuck."

"I know. I know you did. Play me that song, all right?"

He meant it. I stopped the car, slow so as not to jar him. We were in the open country now, and the trees had yellow leaves and red ones and there were red and yellow leaves on the roadside. I took the guitar, mine that had been his, that his salt and his spirit abided in. He wanted his too, so I got it for him, big Nashville Grammer. He could not manage it. He had put his hands on the strings. And he could not do any more. And so then I realized he was not going to make it. Or rather, that he had it made. He had his ticket bought and his train would soon be in. I was thinking I would play a happy song for him. I decided on another one.

"*New River Train*, Tuck. That one okay?"

"Sure, Tyler. That's a good one."

I went ahead with it. Singing it too. The refrain, that same train that brought me here is going to carry me away, and four of the verses, and then the refrain again.

"That's fine, Tyler. Thanks a lot. Let's ride along now, okay? Where'd you say we're going?"

"Hospital, Tuck."

"Okay, then. Let's get on there."

I was driving not very fast, to keep from jolting him. That way I only needed one hand on the wheel, so I kept my other hand and arm in front of him, across his chest, to keep him from swaying. I could have been doing that all the time.

"Ansted?"

"Yessir?"

"You asked me to teach you how to play the guitar once. You remember?"

"Sure, Tuck. I remember that. Best day of my life."

We were at the hospital finally. I went into the emergency room with him. I wanted to find out who it had been. It was the Packers, but it would be better to have direct word.

He would not say who it had been. I could get him to anyway. I was starting to go ahead, when I thought of what he had said. It don't hurt except when you go pushing on me. I had been ready to push on him some more. The first time I met him it was what I had done.

"Well then I did, didn't I, Tyler?"

"Did what, Tuck?"

"Taught you how to play."

"Sure, man. You sure damn did, Tucker. Thanks a lot, you hear?"

"Okay, Tyler." He had a sort of smile. It was not me he was smiling at. "My pleasure, Tyler." Then it was me. "You sure damn learned."

I had to go on out. They were going to take him somewhere and operate. It was not going to matter, and we had said So long, but they had to do something more than let him lay there.

We had been scheduled to play that night, in the town of Winchester. I had some clean clothes, and a razor, in the car. We traveled with a good part of our furnish along. I could change clothes, and shave and wash up, when I got there. Once or twice we had met people, bluegrass bums, some of them good pickers, who lived out of their cars or vans entirely. On the way, I stopped and telephoned Stonefield Smith. His home was over in Romney, West Virginia. He was not in from his job yet. I told his wife there was some work for him tonight, and where I would be, and the telephone number.

In Winchester, the Apple Blossom Lounge, the manager wanted to know why Tuck was not there. I told him Tuck hadn't been able to make it. "Well *you've* got to play, Ansted. I've got to have somebody here. Vance must be really feeling bad, if he doesn't keep an appointment."

"That's Mister Vance."

"Okay. I've never known him to miss one. I don't see how I can pay you the full rate, though. Since it's only going to be the one of you."

"Don't worry about your rate, man."

"Well it's no need to get sore. I just wanted to save us any mis-understanding later."

"Don't worry about your rate."

"Who's worrying? I'm not worrying. You want a soda, maybe? Ginger ale? Nobody's in a rush."

"Let me have a ginger ale, Mr. Baker. Okay?"

"Sure it's okay. Who's worrying?"

At six-thirty, beginning time, I went ahead. In a while, people were asking for requests, and that was a sign the audience was feeling okay. By seven-thirty the place had a fair crowd. Just before eight, Smith came in. Winchester was close to the state line, and his home was only an hour's drive from here. When he saw me by myself he asked me, low, if anything had happened to Tucker, and I told him. I hadn't had a break, but I didn't want one, so I just said to the audience that we were going to have some company now, a fellow some of you already know. Stonefield Smith, friends. He brought his fiddle with him. Stoney Smith. They gave him some applause. I *brung* my fiddle, Tyler. He brung his fiddle, friends. I see you brung your bow too. No, I brought the bow. I couldn't afford the fiddle and bow both at once, Tyler. I got the fiddle first, and by the time I could get the bow I'd been to school and they'd learned me how to talk good. We were making it up. I had not heard him go on like that before. I bet they learned you how to play good too, Stoney. Well no, I can't *play* the fiddle at all. That won't matter, will it, Tyler? Tucker had said not to overdo those things. "You don't want to be sounding slick up there, Ty." Just make some noise with it, Stonefield, if you can't play it. I'll make some with you.

It was nearly two o'clock when we got back to the hospital. The crowd had got bigger, and we had gone ahead and worked it. I was hitting some pretty high notes towards the end. Smith's fiddle stayed in there, driving and driving, bloody and brilliant and right. The special requests kept coming, and we kept playing until the place had to close. We wanted to get enough to get Tucker a gravestone and to cover the other expenses that would come up. I was also going to get a pistol, in case I couldn't find his. At the hospital, he was still alive, but he was not conscious. He had not been conscious since they put him under the anesthetic.

The nurse said we could not go in his room. We went on in. Smith had not seen him for a couple of weeks, and this was the last time he could see him alive. Tucker's face only reminded me of him, now. Most of what had mattered in it was already gone. Before long, we went out. We sat on a bench in the corridor. I had two comics, and we read them, and swapped when we finished. Smith had gone to college for a year, Davis and Elkins College, but he liked comics anyway. Sometime after three, a nurse came out and told us Tucker was dead.

He had a pistol. I went to his room for it. I would need to get Smith started home before I could do anything, but that would not take long. While I was looking for it, though, I found an envelope in a table drawer. It was sealed, but it was marked To Tiler Glasgow Ansted.

From Tucker Vance to Tiler Ansted. Dear Tiler. All the luck to you always, and I trust and believe that God's mercy will follow you every place you go. If anything happens to me, this is my Will since I am in sound mind and body, and all possessions I have I inherit to you. They are my clothes and both of the guitars and the .45. And includeing the Chevy which is part yours anyway since you helped pay for it. If you cannot wear my clothes, which I guess they are too big for you, give them to somebody that can. Or to the Salvation Army since they obliged me when I first got out of the pen. And Tiler nothing is too big for your heart and talent, and therefour I want you to practice every day even if you have a hangover. (Hah.)
Very truly yours, Tucker Renfroe Vance.
P.S. You can keep my initials on your guitar as long as you want to.

The P.S. was in blue ink. The other part was in a darker color. He had done it at a different time than the P.S. I had a good idea of when he had.

On account of the letter, I stopped looking for the pistol. I had meant to take it and go find Stevie Packer. But there had been with them and Tucker blood for blood. And Tucker would not have wanted anymore.

I handed the letter to Smith. In a minute, he gave it back.

"I was going to go see if you wanted to go hunting with me. I don't guess I want to, though."

"I don't want to either, Smith."

"I've got a deerbow and a good rifle in the car. I thought we might do a little hunting."

We could gather up Tucker's belongings later. And mine.

"You think you got room for me at your place tonight, Smith?"

"You bet. Glad to have you."

I didn't want to go back to my own room at any time. It would be necessary to later on, but not tonight.

The funeral was at Mt. Zion. Kenna and two of her kids, and Stonefield, and myself, were there. Tucker's brother got there after it started.

After the funeral, we went to Kenna's house. I was staying there temporarily.

The police already had the man they figured had done the shooting. It was Stevie Packer. The next morning after it happened, he had been in a tavern in South Annistown, drunk and announcing he had done it. They had his pistol, a .38, and the bullet that had been taken out of Tucker's stomach, and the bullet had come from the .38.

Stonefield and I had some wild-grape wine, from his uncle Stinson Smith's place. Last year I had helped him pick the grapes for it. I knew Kenna's views about drinking, though, so we left it in his car. We sat on the porch for a while. She wanted to rest there when we first got back. Kenna was far from young anymore. Smith said Tucker had told him once that after he got out of prison and was back up here, he was despondent, out of hope. "He didn't know where to turn. He heard you playing his guitar at his brother's house one day. He said that was what gave him enough will not to give up yet."

We sat there.

It seemed like all of it had been in the summer. It hadn't, of course, and many times we had put chains on the tires and dogged through the snowdrifts, worked in low gear over the steep roads when they were icing. Four times the leaves had fallen, and four times the green leaves and the redbud and laurel had come again until the hills were frantic with them. I was not going to have any better years. Playing the guitar and singing and working. Meeting those girls and spending time with them and meeting another one. Fighting sometimes. Drinking, and dancing on the broad-board oak. Son, where are you from. Who are you kin to.

"I better get us a little supper together," Kenna said. "You two can set in the kitchen here, if you're a mind to."

We went on in. She told Smith not to feel like he had to do any special way here. She was proud to have him and she wanted him to feel at home. She got some coffee boiling. "I don't know if you have your wife use one of them percolators or not, Mr. Smith. I guess I better go ahead and get one now. Tyler's been away, and I guess he got used to percolator coffee." I told her I couldn't stay away long enough to get used to things she didn't cook.

"Hush, boy. You don't need to be sweet talking me. I'm not one of them spring chickens you chase."

"How did you know I—what makes you think I been chasing any chickens, Aunt Kenna?"

"Hush, boy."

While the coffee was getting ready, she turned around and looked at us for a minute. She said that if it happened we had brought a little something with us, she did not see any strong objections if we brought it on in. She personally never had held with drinking, but she didn't know of any strong objections. Stoney went after it. And when she saw it was wine, she said she might even have a taste herself. She put three glasses on the table. They were from the ones Tucker had got.

She still had a stranger's place set. She was going to invite Stonefield to take that one, but I asked her to put another one down. Whenever she set the table, there was a place that was not used.

Several people around followed that rule. It was in case somebody came by without being expected. Most of her plates used to be cracked or chipped, but she would have a good one instead of a chipped one put at the stranger's place. She had all good ones now. I had sent money from time to time, and her oldest son Arthur Lee had, after he went to the Army last year. When I first brought Tucker to the house, a place at the table was waiting for him. Every time after that when he was here, she left the stranger's place and set another one for him, since she did not want him to be a stranger anymore.

All of his days, that was all he had ever been.

She had made a shirt for me once, and sewed some flags onto the pockets. The shirt was worn out now, and busted out through the shoulders from where I had outgrown it, but I had kept the two Rebel flags, and this morning put them in before the coffin lid was screwed closed. Smith saw me, but he only nodded.

We talked about the future. She wanted to know why Smith and me didn't get up another band, three or four people. He had had his troubles with bands. I went ahead anyway and said Why don't we.

"Okay, Ansted. Why the hell don't we?"

He had a wife and kid, and his job was the only sure way he had for them.

"I ain't hardly forgot it, Ty. I think I'll just take my chances anyway."

He had a cousin named Norine. She had sung with a band before she got married. Sometimes a band did better if a girl was in it. He said she would probably sing with us if she did not have to spend too much time away from her kids, traveling.

Having a band would mean a lot of managing. Taking things into account. How this one's husband would feel about her being in public so much. Making sure that one was ready to go in time.

"Here's the main thing, Tyler. Do you want to have one?"

"Nothing else besides. I'm going to do it."

"All right then. You're ready for it, seems like to me. You been ready. Tucker's already got you housebroke. He said once it would be easier housebreaking a hellcat. He told me—." He looked at

Kenna, but she was over by the stove, stirring something. She took some bread out of the oven. The smell it gave was like complicated chords when they got resolved. "He told me once if he'd let you, you'd spent half your time in the back of that station wagon and the other half with Old Forester."

"Well I'll be Goddamn. I wore my fingers raw, practicing. I looked at music till I couldn't see the notes straight."

"I know you did. Settle down. He was bragging about you, man. He bragged about you two or three times. He don't have much use for people that mind easy. Didn't have. But I'll manage the thing, okay? I managed that Ridge Runners outfit, and they were going for nearly a year. They'd still be going, if they'd held on. But you'll go down the line for something, Tyler. Just like Tucker did. I will too. For this I will."

Tucker Renfroe Vance.

If I had let him stay in the car agency, he could still be there.

Kenna gave something from the Bible once that she said she didn't understand. The living dog is better than the dead lion.

The ones that wanted to believe that, they were welcome to.

We talked about names for the band. We settled for Jack's Mountain Hoboes. That would include Tucker, since sometimes he liked for me to drive him to a place up on Jack's Mountain. I would stop the car at an overlook, and we would sit there for a while. Way out on the mountain.

"We can get to something with this, Tyler. You have star-stink on you. You don't smell, I don't mean that, but if it was something they have a name for, that's the one it would be. The other night. In that Apple Blossom Lounge? It was pouring off you."

In the prison, they had whipped him. But what they had to get to was the soul. And their writ didn't run that far.

Kenna wanted us to do some playing while we were there. She said that in the old days, people would have singing and music at funerals. Her grandmother had told her how her great-great-grandmother said people always had singing when somebody had died. That was years back, in another part of the world, before the first Camerons and the first Ansteds and Renfroes and Glasgows that came over here in ships did come over. When a person had died and he was on his way home, music was thought to guard him from evil things on the way. People would drink, and have singing together, and tell how the dead person had always faced up to his troubles and the friendly things he had done. All that might be only old people's notions, but some music couldn't do any harm.

I got up. Smith did too. "Come on, Smith. We'll get him home."

We went out to the car, for the instruments. Coming back, though, on the porch, I told him to go ahead. He looked at me, and I looked at him, except maybe by that time I could not see clear, and he went on in.

I brushed at my eyes, so as to see. It was moonlight now, and the letters on the guitar were shining. My hand was wet, and I used that to shine them some more.

There was a time, when he might have wanted to keep working for the car place. But when he was called on, by me, he made the choice he did make. The time might come for me, if I was lucky it would, when I would be asked, as that day I had called on him. He had said once, that the furrow had been started and he would plow to the end of it. He had not turned aside, and so maybe neither would I.

And whether one way or some other, there would not be, for him, any lessening. Or any lessening of what we had had. No matter what I would fall short of, or go too far with.

I touched the letters on the guitar. The ends of my fingers had thick callouses, from the playing. Particles of steel from the strings could work into the callousing, and through the inner layers, and draw to the bone. Gold was stronger than steel, and so maybe some of it would draw to the bone.

I did not need to do any shining of those letters. They were glinting now, in the harvest light, but he had already given his name all it needed. It was shined with his own losing and winning and enduring, the years, when during all of them he wore his mortality like it was some expensive best style until somebody did him the favor, which he no way wanted, of being his valet and taking it off for him.

Kenna, and my brother Stonefield, were at the table in the lighted kitchen. They had some wine, and a glass was waiting for me. They were waiting, but they were not impatient. I would go on inside now. Drink the wine with them, and pour another glass. And get the guitar tuned, and begin with some music.

In the City

Four-thirty again, and Shelby was on his way home again, through for the day. This job, he delivered groceries for the Hermitage Food Mart. It was easy work, as work went, mainly pedaling a bicycle and climbing stairs with bags and cartons. Not that any of it was any good. The manager had asked him at the interview why he wanted to work in the Hermitage organization. He didn't want to at all, but he was still making payments on his guitar back then, so he had to work somewhere.

This was the third week of it now. The manager had told him the other day he had got the job because of his appearance. "You have an honest face, Shelby. I notice too that you definitely have a clean-cut way about you. I had to turn down several who approached me about working here. I do not understand how people suppose they can get anywhere with their hair down to their shoulders." He more or less stayed clean, and he had also let him mother give him a haircut the night before he applied for the job. She worked in beauty parlors, off and on, and she could cut hair good when she was unjuiced.

He liked the getting-off-from-work sensation the job had. His feet and ankles kept wanting to go up and down by themselves, on account of the bicycle riding. That was probably part of how it felt to be drunk. He used to shine shoes, and a good many of his customers had been under the affluence. The way his old lady walked sometimes, when she was making it in from Kay's, she looked like she enjoyed the way her feet and ankles performed. Aside from that, steering the bicycle, and carrying the groceries, built up the wrist muscles, and for guitar playing you needed strong wrists. Shoeshining did the same thing, but he had thrown his supplies, cans and bottles and brushes and the box he carried them in, at a customer one night, and that had been the end of the shoeshining. Callouses had built up on his knees, from the kneeling he had done on sidewalks and on floors of bars and lounges where the customers were.

But he had the guitar now. It was paid for. One hundred and ten dollars. He had got it from Eastman's Loans, over in the honkytonk section. Weekly payments, four dollars and five dollars and one week when business had been extra good, tourists in town for the Grand Ole Opry and for an extra thrill getting their shoes shined, a full twelve. The guitar had stayed in the back room at Eastman's, tagged with his name, Shelby Tullahoma Deaderick, during the months he was paying for it. The day came when he made the last payment. He had a dollar and some change left, and he used that to buy a case for it. That was the last money he had, at the time, but a guitar needed to be provided with a case. He was broke when he walked out of Eastman's, but he was walking out with his guitar, and it was in a case.

The extensor digitorum muscle. The carpi ulnaris. They were the main ones, in the wrists. Since they were working for him it was a good idea to know their names. He had been checking in the library for books about sex, and found some about anatomy in general. Anatomy was almost as interesting as sex. An embryo looked like the bass clef symbol in music. Big head, nearly all of it head, the rest just a curl. Anatomy was on the order of notation for music. Sex was like the music itself. It probably was. He didn't know all that much about it yet, but he was pretty sure it was.

When he was shoeshining, he had heard plenty of music. Where he worked then was in the honkytonk part of town, Commerce Street and lower Broadway and around the bus stations, and he worked mostly at night. Since they had to live in the city now, at least it was this one, Nashville, Music City, and that part of town was crawling with music people. Pickers, drummers, hogcallers, all kinds. His new

job was in the daytime, and it didn't have much music. The pay was
better, though, and it was regular pay. He could also get an apple or
a candy bar between deliveries, or a carton of milk. The manager
cried like a baby when he took milk. It cost more than candy. He
took it anyway, since it had calcium and vitamins and he wanted his
teeth to stay good. A performer, that had an audience watching him,
either had to have natural good-looking teeth or else spend a holy
fortune getting them made good-looking. By luck he already had
good ones. He had inherited good-teeth genes from Deaderick. From
his old man. Deaderick had cut out a few years ago, but he had been
back two or three times, and he had noticed how white the man's
teeth were. He was the only kid Deaderick and his old lady had had.
They had not been married, so he was sort of illegitimate, a bastard
as far as that went, but Deaderick was still his old man. He would
probably also have some weight, like Deaderick, later on. Deaderick
was a bruiser. He already weighed one fifty, none of it blubber, and
he was only fifteen. His mother said fifteen, but Deaderick's figuring
would make him sixteen. He mainly took Deaderick's opinion about
it.

Besides the regular pay, he got tips sometimes, from people he
delivered to. Some of the women put good tips on him. One of them
gave him seventy-five cents each time. She ought to. He had to carry
her edibles three flights up, with the bike, that belonged to
Hermitage, in the alley where it could be stolen. It had a lock on the
rear wheel and one for the cover of its sidecar, but they didn't mean
much. He could pick an average lock himself in a couple of minutes.
He had learned how from his stepfather. So far, though, the bike
locks had not been tampered with.

He was in his own neighborhood now. The streets here did not
have much traffic, but they still felt crowded, and they were hot. A
good many of the houses here were big ones, brick, with big yards.
Most of the big ones were boarded up, or they had four or five
families. The others were small ones, like the one he lived in. Crates,
close to the sidewalk.

Dale Raleigh's house was a crate. It was the one he was passing
now. It was not actually the Raleigh house anymore, since they had

moved away. They had been here when his own family moved here from the country, three years ago. He and Dale had got to be partners. Dale was the one he had learned the basic guitar chords from. Dale had been carried to the hospital one night, though, too many speed pills or something. The Raleighs had moved soon after Dale died. Nobody lived in their house now. He had not got to know anybody else in the neighborhood, beyond knowing their names. The first playing he did with his guitar, though, before he got home with it, he turned in at Dale's house on his way, and went around to the back, and picked for a while there. *Three o'clock in the morning, moonlight bright as day.* Just those two bars, blues, and some variations on them, on the back steps where weeds were growing.

The Hall of Fame Pantry Grocery. Meat & Groc. Goods. He would stop in there, and get some stuff to take home.

Ransom came around the corner. Saw him, and started hurrying to meet him.

Ransom Pugh. His stepbrother. His mother had four other kids besides him. Their father, his stepfather, was in jail.

"Randy."

"Shelby. How's it going?"

"Where you headed, Randy? Come on in the grocery with me."

"You bet, Shelby. I'll be glad to."

He was not always friendly this way with Randy. It made him ashamed to see how happy Randy was now that he was being friendly.

He had learned about locks from Ransom's father. Pugh had picked some he should have left unpicked. Three years for it. One was finished, two left. Ransom was the oldest one of the kids. Nine years old. Then two girls, and then another boy.

The Pantry Grocery was in a basement. The steps down into it from the sidewalk had wear hollows in them. They were concrete, but each one was scooped out in the middle from use over the years and years. Steps only got worn that way when they were used by people with worries. People with burdens who had to keep going anyway. One man he saw in here sometimes, a young man, was deaf and had an artificial larynx and two artificial hands. It was from what had happened to him in Vietnam. There was not going to be any music whatever for that man.

The place was chilly inside. Airconditioned.

"We going to need a cart, Shelby?"

"Not getting that much. I don't guess we are. What do we need?"

"Will you get some pork chops, Shelby? Can you?"

"Sure. I guess we can rip off a few pork chops."

Rice. Onions. Tomato sauce. Bread.

They were at the cold-drink case.

"Shelby? Can I have a soda? You got that much change?"

Milk would be better for him. It was a soda he wanted, though. Sweaty day. Randy was already looking disappointed, making the maneuvers in his eyes that were supposed to keep the disappointment from showing.

"Go ahead and get you one. Want a big one? Get one of them twenty-five-cent ones."

"Hey. You're a real pal, Shelby."

"Sure, man. I'm the last of the big spenders."

Randy picked out a can of ginger ale. Pulled the tab off. Drank, and kept drinking. Stopped finally. His eyes were blinking. "Man. Man, is that ever good. You take a swallow, Shelby. Take all you want."

He took some. It was in fact good. Cold. Cold.

"Let's get on to the house, Randy. I'll play you something. You like to hear *Davy Crockett?*"

"No kidding. Will you play that—."

"What's the matter?"

No answer.

"What are you looking like that for? You hear me? You look here at me."

"She sold it, Shelby."

"Sold what? Who did? What did she sell? Don't you lie to me, Ransom."

"Your guitar, Shelby. Mama sold it."

Ransom stumbled away. He had hit him. The ginger ale can fell on the floor.

"You lying to me? If you are, boy, I'll hit you harder than that."

Ransom was not lying. He would pester you for cold drinks, try to follow you around when you wanted to be by yourself, but he didn't lie. If only he did. This time anyway, if only he did.

"What did you do with it?"

She looked scared. "Do with what, Shelby?"

"Where is it?" He could still get it back. Find whoever had it, get it back.

"Shelby. Wait, now. Listen, wait, Shelby. Let me explain it to you."

They were in the kitchen. A half-pint bottle on the table. Vodka. Empty.

"Is that what you did with it? A damn little half a pint of vodka."

"Shelby. Shelby, listen to me."

"Who's got it? Did you sell it to somebody? Did you pawn it? Where is it?"

He didn't want to be talking this way to her. Swearing at her, hollering. He had not so far actually done any swearing at her, but it felt like he had. She was looking like he had.

"I don't know, Shelby. I'd tell you, I really would, if I knew. It was this gentleman in Kay's. I didn't know him, if I did I'd tell you, believe me I would. You believe me, don't you, Shelby? You do, don't you?"

He managed not to make any answer. Not any to make. Not to have any. Not any to have.

She was beginning to be weepy. Most times that meant she would soon be getting dramatic. She must have had more than half a pint. The half pint was only added on to what she had already had. Two dollars. That was what half a pint cost.

"Don't you look at me like that, young man. Let me tell you something. Don't you dare look at me like that."

She was dramatic already. Then, she surprised him. "I know that Deaderick look. How well I know it. How many times have I not observed him cast his regard on me like that. Dirt under his feet. My heart and soul, Christ knows he was. And you think I made any difference to him? Your father, that's the one I'm talking about. Don't think I don't know where you got that Deaderick look. Don't think for a minute I don't."

A pretty woman. He had a sort of recollection of when she had been much more than pretty. Even now, no matter that she got upset so easy and was starting to weigh too much, some of what had been there was still there. Once, one of the times his father was here, he had woke up one night. Her voice. Pleading, and she had been saying, Be finished with me. You promised you wouldn't come back, and here you are.

Maybe he was only fifteen after all.

Ransom came in. He had a bag of groceries. What they had got at the store. He had left Ransom there, and cut out.

She got up. Stumbled. Put a hand on the table, and got her balance again. Really loaded.

"How am I ever going to get out of this pigpen."

"Shelby. Shelby, I'm sorry, you hear? I swear it on the Bible I am. If I only hadn't done it."

The other kids, the two girls, were giggling. They got nervous, along in these incidents. The baby was trying to get Ransom to take the groceries out of the bag. Not a baby anymore. Five years old. Doug. Pugh had a lot of respect for Douglas McArthur, and the youngest kid was named Douglas MacArthur Pugh. His nickname was General.

Ransom was saying something. Asking if they could take the groceries out. He told Ransom to go ahead.

He had money in his pocket. Not much, but some. He could have given her two bucks, and still had enough for groceries.

He was in his room. On his bed. Dark, now. It had been dark for a long time. Ransom was in the room. He had not been asleep exactly, but he did not know when Ransom had come in.

"Shelby? How you doing? You awake?"

He wished Ransom would go on away.

"Mama cried for a long time. She's gone to sleep."

It sounded like Ransom expected him to make some kind of answer.

"You want me to do anything for you, Shelby?"

Ransom, he knew, was trying to be friendly. The odd thing, somebody else had said almost the same words. Last month, on Cee Street, Royal somebody, one of the people that hung out in the Cee Street places. Is there anything you would like me to do for you, Shellaby? He had just finished shining Royal's shoes. He threw the box and brushes and bottles at Royal, and went on away. Not hurrying. Not looking back. Some of the polish was liquid, and from the way it was moving through the air it was going to splash on Royal's shirt, a ruffled one with long droopy sleeves, for show business a workshirt, but he never knew if it did. In a way, even at the time, he wished he hadn't done it. Royal was a musician. Not much of one, but still a musician. He played a zither. He had a habit of telling people that his days on earth were going to be brief. In the Cee Street bars, gay places, he would tell tourists he had cancer. "I'm afraid I only have a brief time remaining." They would give him tips then, and ask for his autograph.

"Shelby? You hear?"

"No. Except let me alone or something. Just go on away, all right? And let me alone."

Randy looked at him. He looked back to let Randy know he meant it.

Ransom got up. Was leaving.

At the door, he stopped.

"All right, go on." He turned towards the wall, and closed his eyes. Maybe he would go on to sleep.

Things had never been like this when they lived in the country. If they could only someday get back, it wouldn't be like this then. But they were not going to get back.

After a time, he realized that Ransom had not left yet. He was facing the wall, and he had shut his eyes, but he knew anyhow that Ransom was still in the doorway. He rolled over, to tell Ransom again, this time in a way that would get him the hell on out, to go ahead and leave. But then, he changed his mind.

"All right. All right, come on back in. Don't hang around in the door anyway. Come on back in, okay?"

Ransom came back in. And in a minute, sat down.

He looked at Ransom. "Think you're smart, don't you, buddy?"

"Hell, Shelby."

In a bad time, Ransom was the one who had stayed around. Who would not be driven away. And he resolved that he would not, as long as he ever lived, forget it.

"Shelby? You don't really think we're pigs, do you?"

"What? Certainly not. What made you say that?"

"Well, you said how were you ever going to get out of this pigpen. And you can play so good, and we're just your half brothers and sisters."

"I can't play good, Ransom. Not yet anyway."

"Yes you can, Shelby. You won that contest in school that time. And you got the blue ribbon on that radio show for kids. I think you can sing good, too."

"Okay. But listen. You're not just my half brother. We've got different names, sure, but that don't matter. To me it don't. You're my brother, Ransom. Never mind about the names."

"Right, Shelby."

"I mean it, you hear? Don't you talk like that no more, either. Things are bad enough as it is."

"Yessir. I mean, okay. I won't, Shelby. Right on. Listen. I'll help you get another one, if you want me to. Another guitar. I can do shoeshining. And you can have all I make. And counting what you make too, it wouldn't be long till you got another one."

"You know how long it took me for that one? Seven months and a week. Oh well. Thanks anyway, Randy. It's okay."

They left off talking. He thought he might be going to sleep.

And later, it turned out that he had in fact been sleeping. Maybe for a long time. Things felt late. He was rested, now. Peaceful. And he knew, now, what he was going to do.

Ransom was still there. Twisted up asleep, in the armchair by the bed. A little bass clef symbol.

By the kitchen clock it was only ten-thirty. Not late after all. What he wanted, Pugh's kit of tools, was here in the kitchen. In the storage cabinet, out of sight behind some other things.

A metal case. Inside, it had probes and lock cylinders and master keys, neat and in rows on felt-covered trays. A miniature electric drill, with a set of carbide bits that would go into steel. A bottle of cooling oil, so the bits would not overheat. Pugh had worked on government projects once or twice, when the government wanted something. There was a screwdriver with a flexible shaft. Some files. A dental mirror. All in order.

He found he was hungry. He never had got any supper. He made himself a sandwich. Ham and mustard, two of them, and sat down.

A newspaper, part of one, on the table. The front page. Local Executive Alleged Cocaine Middleman. White House Mum on Break Ins, Burglaries. Abandoned Newborn Boy Found In Centennial Park. Cheerful news these days.

Local Man Killed By Police In Break In. An Edgehill area man was shot to death yesterday by a Metro policeman minutes after he and a companion robbed a furniture store on Broad Street. His companion, also shot, but not fatally, is being treated in.

Ransom came in. "Shelby." He yawned, and sat down. "What have you got my Dad's tool kit for, Shelby?" He was awake, then. Wide awake. "Hey. Shelby. What are you fixing to do?"

"Quiet down. You'll wake people up."

"Excuse me. What are you fixing to do?"

"You want to hear *Davy Crockett*, don't you? All right, you'll hear *Davy Crockett.*"

"Shelby. Listen. Let me go with you, Shelby."

Ransom was serious. Why not take him up on it.

Better off without a companion.

"No, man. Nothing doing."

Ransom started to argue.

"I told you, all right? Nothing doing."

He stopped arguing.

"You ever get any supper, Randy?"

"Sure. We had a lot of supper. I think I'll have another sandwich, though. Since we're in here."

"How did you work it to get these groceries, Randy? I kind of ran out on you, in the store."

"Mr. Vince let me put them on ticket. I though you knew we had a ticket there."

"Oh. I guess I knew it, sure."

They ate their sandwiches for a while.

There was something he had better say. Maybe better not.

"You're thinking about something, aren't you, Shelby?"

"Not actually. The thing is, though, if anything goes wrong, I didn't mean to smack you the way I did. In the store back there. Okay?"

"That's all right, Shelby. Bygones is bygones. It won't nothing go wrong."

In a minute, Ransom got up. When he came back he had the guitar case.

Mosely's Instruments. Dim, in here. Stuffy.

A small place. It was on a side street, where there was not much coming and going even during the daytime. Only enough light in here to let him make out the different objects. Violins and violas and cellos. Flat-top guitars and electrics, mandolins also and dulcimers, a balalaika. Even their names could ruin you. It was like sitting on the back porch of Dale Raleigh's empty house. Like Ransom asking for a cold drink.

New instruments. They would be smooth to the touch, if he went ahead and touched any. Healing to the eye, the retinas in his eyes and the channel nerves into the brain. Instruments that had never belonged to anybody. They were waiting, in case their owners came along. It might turn out to be only their purchasers instead of their owners, and all the waiting would be for nothing.

There was something he could do. He could merely go ahead and leave. Take himself on out of here, and let the instruments stay as they were, let the carpi ulnaris and the rest go their own way. Or he could do what he thought at first he had come here to do. He could pick one thing, or the other.

It came to him that it was his mother who had made it possible for him to be in this situation. The thing that was beautiful about it was that it would not matter which one he did. Something would come of it if he did one thing, but something else would if he did the other. Sometimes he saw people like Merle Haggard, Tyler Ansted, Mel Tillis that stuttered so bad and sang so good. They lived in town here, or came here to make records. They must have been many times in situations like the one he was in now. Where they had to decide and knew ahead of time it would not matter. That was the reason, he knew now, they had such friendly blasted eyes. Once he had shined Tyler Ansted's shoes. When he finished, and stood up, Tyler Ansted saw that he had recognized him, and they nodded to each other. Their eyes met, and it became clear to him that Tyler Ansted would have seen how it was about having to be in the city, about the steps at the grocery store and the broken people and the well ones who went up and down them, and up and down them, and up and down them. Tyler paid him fifty cents for the shine. The regular rate. He would permit him to shine his shoes, but not for nothing. It was a good lesson. When the time came that somebody would be shining his own shoes, he would know not to let them do it for nothing and also not to give them more than it was worth. Then, though, he realized that there was no permitting involved. Tyler Ansted just wanted his shoes shined, and he happened to be there with his shine kit.

He could decide. So he went ahead eventually, and decided.

Outside again, with the guitar case heavy now. He went to the corner. Lower Broadway, where the honkytonks were, was on his left, downhill. That was his old territory. There was a bus stop down there. It was getting late. He had better take a bus back home. A long way.

Before he got to the bus stop, a Metro car, a police cruiser, came along. Stopped. The two cops in it were looking him over. He did not recognize the driver, but the other one was Felix the Fuzz. He knew Felix from his shoeshining days.

Felix called to him. "Hey, boy. Don't you think it's kind of late for you to be out?"

"I'm heading in right now."

"About time you were."

"Give me a ride home, Felix. Okay?"

"Ride, hell." Felix winked at him. "You get your rear end on home, Deaderick. You hear me, now." The patrol car was moving again. It went on.

Half a block from the bus corner, he met Royal. Royal was standing in front of the Kitty Kat. Greeting him. At first, he wished he had not met up with Royal again. Then, it was all right.

"Why Shellaby! My little hoodlum!"

Music was coming out of the Kitty Kat. Out of the other places in this block. A liquor store across the street. A lot of red and green and lavender neon. Popcorn smells. Hamburger and onion smells. Two men and two women came along. They looked like they were from out of town. One of the women was talking. Well I declare I just love it here in Music City. We just don't have anything in Atlanter like this at all.

"How have you been, Shellaby? I haven't seen you for quite a while now."

Royal was not a bad guy. He himself might have a few things to think over, considering how excited he had got the last time he had seen Royal. There was one old guy, a crippled old derelict, that used to be around here. Every day, Royal would buy him food.

"I been pretty good, Royal. How's yourself? Listen. I wonder if you'd do something for me?"

In the morning, when his mother woke up, she was probably going to be sick.

"Well of course, Shellaby. Anything at all."

She had done a lot for him. He could do something in return. He knew what she was going to need.

"Well listen, Sport. Take this two bucks and go across the street over there and get me a half pint of vodka. I mean if you don't mind. Okay?"

Hundred to One

Lee had an idea what car it was as soon as he heard it stop, and when he looked out the window he saw that it was in fact the Welfare car. It was the grey station wagon that Mrs. Bimmelson from Welfare drove. This time Mrs. Bimmelson had somebody with her, a man Lee did not know. Since she had the strange man along, he figured that this time she had come to do what she had been saying she might have to do. She meant to take him this time, and Marilyn and Marcia with him.

They were his sisters, and if they had been indoors, or in the back-yard, he could have got them out of sight, and kept Bimmelson from getting them, or him either. But they were in the front yard. Marcia was holding up her left arm, to show Mrs. Bimmelson. She had sprained her wrist last week, and it had splints on it.

They had been playing with their doll. It was the one he had got them in January, when he had been working at the Doughnut Dock. He had meant to get them a doll each, but his father had taken three bucks of his money without letting him know, and that only left enough for one. They were watching Mrs. B now, and the man with her. Mrs. B and the man went on towards the front door. Marcia was still holding up her arm. They hadn't seemed to notice her. They were people who had things to do.

He went to the front door, and turned the catch that locked it. Bimmelson had once just come on in, without knocking. This time she would have to knock.

She did. Loud. He let her go ahead a few times. That would scare his mother, though, and he unlocked the door, and opened it.

"You rang, Madam?"

"Is your mother in the house, Leland?" They moved towards him. They expected him to stand aside. He didn't, and they had to stop. It got them agitated. He did stand aside then, and they went on in, through the living room and into his mother's room.

His mother was lying down. He could not tell if she recognized Mrs. Bimmelson. She had got to a place where she could be, a little, out of things. He was glad. It was a break for her. The only trouble, sometimes it took her a minute when she woke up before she recognized him either.

"Mom? Mrs. Bimmelson's here."

She was just lying there. On top of the covers, her arms quiet along her sides. She herself had put fresh sheets and a fresh blanket on her bed this morning. Maybe she was better. Lately, he had been needing to do that.

"Cora." Mrs. Bimmelson's voice was loud. "Mrs. Langley! This is Mrs. Bimmelson, Mrs. Langley."

He told her to stop yelling. "It scares her when you yell at her."

"This is Mrs. Bimmelson, Cora. How are we this afternoon?"

"Oh, I think about the same. How are you, Mrs. Bimmelson?"

"This is Mrs. Bimmelson, Cora."

"Will you stop yelling at her?"

The man with Mrs. Bimmelson looked at him. "All right. Enough of that."

Marilyn and Marcia were standing in the doorway. Close together. Their eyes were big.

Mrs. Bimmelson was opening her briefcase. She was panting. She was fat, and talking got her out of breath, even when she didn't yell.

"Cora, there's some things I need to discuss with you this afternoon."

There was a chair here in the bedroom. She was Mrs. B, but he could ask her to sit down anyway. He brought the chair over. She put herself down on it.

"This is Mr. Fisher, Cora. From Juvenile Protection? Leland, is David here?"

"You mean my father?"

"Now, Leland, who else could I mean?"

Sometimes she called his mother Mrs. Langley. She never said Mr. Langley for his father.

She took an envelope out of her briefcase, and took a paper out of the envelope. A long sheet, with typewriting on it. Domestic Court, Davidson County. Some signatures at the bottom.

"I hope you won't be too upset about this, Cora. We've discussed this at previous times before, I'm sure you remember. I wish it hadn't become necessary to do this. But for the best interests of all concerned, it's what I'm afraid we must do. I'll just read this out to you, Cora. Try and concentrate, please, so I can read it to you."

What he heard, as he went out the window, was the sound his mother made. It was No. Loud, drawn out, the first sound that was loud that he had heard her make for a long time, and then it turned into his name, Leland, and that was drawn out too. She never called him Leland except when something was the matter.

He was out the window by then, bathroom window, and on the ground. He cut around the house, and through the back yard.

At the fence, he stopped, and looked back. That Fisher bastard was already on the kitchen porch. Fisher was smart. Fisher must have guessed he would go through the back yard, instead of out to the sidewalk. He waved to Fisher, and put his hands on the top edge of the fence, and swung himself over. He stayed ducked down, out of sight so Fisher could not see which way he was going, and ran along the alley. Up to the next street, and turned left. He had not figured it out beforehand, but that was the out-of-town direction.

On the street, he stopped running. If he ran, it would attract attention. He was winded, anyway. For the next few minutes he might as well take it easy.

After Bimmelson had finished reading the paper, a court order, he realized that he and Marilyn and Marcia would in fact have to go with her. She didn't want to do any talking about it. "Really, there's no point in we discussing this, Cora." But what the paper said he had to do and what he was going to do, was different. So he said he had to go to the bathroom.

Fisher said Hurry it up, sonny. Mrs. Bimmelson said Leland, will you please not take too long. When he was in, he locked the door. But when he tried to open the window, it would not move. Dampness had made the wood swell. Or something, and his right hand didn't have all its strength anymore either. By the time he got the window unstuck, Fisher must have realized what he was up to. Fisher was banging at the door. The towel bracket was sticking out, from the window frame, and when he went through he tore his shirt. And got a scrape along his ribs from it. All the same, he had got through. Out the window and gone.

Fisher might call the cops, but maybe he would be out of town first. The city limits line was only a mile away. When he got across, the city cops couldn't do anything. The court order wouldn't work either.

He knew some people out in the country. A family named Baring. Mr. Baring and his father were old friends. Or anyway they used to be. From when they had been in Korea. If he could make it to their house, he would visit them.

First, though, he had to sit down. The only place was out here in public, but he sat down anyway, on the curb. There was a mailbox, and that gave him something to lean his head against. If anybody wanted to know what he was doing, he would tell them he had come here to mail a letter and he was resting. A heavy letter.

He wondered where his father might be. Not that it mattered much. His father had left the house early last night, and had not got back.

He would not know where Marilyn and Marcia were going to be. Bimmelson had refused to say. The way Welfare did when it put kids somewhere, it wouldn't let the parents know. A fellow he had known when he was still in school had been put in a foster home, and hadn't been able to see any of his family for six months. Arjay Sutton. That was the fellow's name. Arjay Sutton said he had been climbing the walls sometimes, wanting to see them.

He couldn't go back to the house. Fisher, or else the police, would be there. But his mother couldn't take care of herself. She had been getting better lately, but she was not that much better.

He had a little money in his pocket. Two quarters, and some nickels and pennies. There was a grocery store two blocks over. He could get a tube of glue in that store. It only cost thirty-nine cents. He never had done that, glue-blowing, but he knew people that had, and they said it was a good deal. It lasted for hours, and the whole time you wouldn't care about anything.

Blowing glue rotted your brain cells. If you had any that were not already rotted.

His right hand began hurting. It already had been, and now he was noticing it. He had been pushing hard to get the window open. The knuckles on that hand were crooked. He had banged it against a door one day. Two years ago. One afternoon, something his mother said. "Aren't things ever going to let up? Lee, aren't we ever going to be worth anything? Have anything?" That was when it came to him that they probably were not. It was approximately a hundred to one they were not. He tried to get in the cellar. The house they lived in that time had one, and for some reason that was where he wanted to get. The door was locked, and he banged his fist for a few minutes against the boards. Since then, his right hand didn't have the grip it used to.

Afterwhile, he got up. The letter had been heavy, but he was rested now, thanks. And started walking again. It felt like he had heard somebody say that before. About being rested. In a minute, he remembered. Mr. Baring had said it. Mr. Baring had been shot, in Korea one night, and his father had carried him until they got to a safe place. It was Mr. Baring who had told about it. "And when I asked your Daddy if I was heavy, you see, in the hospital afterwards, he said yes, you were heavy, but I'm rested now, thanks. Hurt? Jesus God. I started asking him finally just to put me down and leave me there, so it would stop hurting maybe. He wouldn't though."

It was five miles to the Baring house. Maybe he would get a ride, once he got out of town. If he didn't, then he would have to walk it.

Mrs. Baring was putting supper on the table when he got there. "Well would you look who's here! Leland Langley! How are you, lover? Come on in, Lee. Come on in this house."

She said she would set a place for him, and he could sit down and eat some supper with them.

He was already sitting down, in a chair by the wall.

"Would you like to wash up a little bit, Lee? It won't all be ready for a few minutes yet. Lee? Oh. You just want to sit there and take it easy a while, don't you? You go right ahead, then. You go right ahead."

After a time, he felt all right. She gave him a look, but he felt okay, and he went ahead and got washed up.

She had chicken stew for supper, and noodles. When he finished one plate of it, she filled his plate again. "My Lord, Lee. You've lost weight since the last time I even saw you. But you came to the right place, at least. Linda, will you pass Lee the bread? Wait a minute, lover, so I can put some butter on it for you. Here."

It was hard to finish the second plateful. He got it finished anyway. The trouble was how his mother would make out for supper. There was food in the house, but she might not bother. At one time, she didn't much care about eating anything even after he had fixed it.

Mrs. Baring and the children, Linda and Alvin and two younger kids, were the only ones there. Skippy Baring, Mr. Baring, was over in Shelbyville. Davy was with him. Davy was the oldest kid. He was nineteen, though. Not a kid anymore. They were setting floor tile in a new house, and they would not be home until late.

Mr. Baring was a sort of contractor. When he was not setting tile he was putting in insulation, or painting, or fixing roofs, or nailing up siding. All the things combined, they made a way to get by.

Once, his father and Skippy Baring had worked on some of those jobs together. Skippy's son Davy was named David, after his father. A long time back, his father and Mr. Baring had had an auto body shop back in town. When they had to close it up, his father worked in a garage. And after that in filling stations around town. As a car jockey in parking lots. Caddying, at the Country Club. His father had medals from Korea, and he had had to be a golf caddy. The income he had that could be counted on anymore was his pension from

Korea. Sixty-eight dollars a month, for partial loss of hearing. When he first got back from Korea, he had had to be in a mental hospital for three months. The Army said the mental condition was over with, though, and he only had a loss-of-hearing pension. Times had come when he had been cashing a lot of the pension checks in bars. This past year was one of those times. Spending them where he cashed them.

The Baring family. Other families. Arjay Sutton's. Most of the families he knew about were like his own and Sutton's. Bimmelson had a good deal of trade in his part of town.

If he could only have kept working at the Doughnut Dock, she would not have been at the house today. The man that owned the place had wanted somebody older, though. He had only been fifteen back then. There could still be a way out. He had been promised a job that would start next Monday, at Brent's Service Station. That was only three days away. He had turned sixteen now, and the age would not make that much difference anymore. And if his father would start using the checks in the house again, things would not be so bad at all. But Mrs. Bimmelson had said that could not be counted on.

After supper, the rest of them watched TV, and Mrs. Baring mended his torn shirt. She had him put on one of Alvin's. When he did, she saw the raw mark on his ribs.

"Did David do that to you? Your father?"

He had already told her about Bimmelson and Fisher. He told her then how he go the scratch. There was no need for her to think his father had done something he hadn't.

Mr. Baring and Davy got in just before nine. Mr. Baring shook hands with him, and Davy scrubbed a hand over his head. Davy was going to be drafted next month. Mrs. Baring had mentioned it earlier. She dreaded it. He would almost certainly be sent to Vietnam, she said. The other kids were pulling at Mr. Baring then, and wanting to know if he had brought them anything. He had some M & M's for them. Alvin went to the kitchen and brought back two cans of beer. Alvin himself was not allowed to have beer. He drank some out of Davy's can anyway. Davy caught him, and poured a little of the beer down Alvin's neck.

Mr. Baring had tiredness lines in his face. He was not a young man anymore. He had put in a long day's work.

David and Mr. Baring went on into the kitchen, to eat. The other kids started to follow them, but Mrs. Baring sent them back. She said she wanted to talk to their father.

A little later, Skippy asked him if he wanted to go back in town. Skippy and Mrs. Baring both were going, and she said maybe he ought to just stay here. But he did want to go back. He had already put on his own shirt again. He was going to stay, when he got back. The court order couldn't touch him out here, and it could in town, but he was going to stay anyway. Visiting the Barings had been a break, but the break was over.

His mother was awake, and up, when they got to the house. She called through the door before she opened it, Who is it? When he told her, the door went open and she had met him before he had time to go through. She didn't say anything. She just held to him.

He brought an extra chair into the living room, and she had the Barings sit down. It was the same one he had offered Mrs. Bimmelson. Only this afternoon. It seemed like a long time back.

There was something peculiar about the house. It was Marcia and Marilyn not being here. Caved-in. All these hours, she had been here by herself.

In the living room, they were talking away, and then, she said they had better be a little quiet. His father was here, and she didn't want to wake him up. He looked at her.

"He's perfectly all right," she said. "He just didn't feel well, is all. And he looked just exhausted, he really did.—But I'm *so* glad you came by." She was speaking to the Barings again. "I was sitting here, you know. And then I heard somebody knock on the door. And here you were!"

Perfectly all right. She meant his father had come in sober. How about that.

There had been a different time. There was a picture somewhere in the house of his father in uniform. Not much older than Davy Baring was now. Sergeant's stripes. "David Langley." Husky, smiling a little. A person somebody would like to know. That they would want to name their oldest son after.

"When did he get here, Mom?"

"Your father? About nine, I think. I tried to get him to stay up a while, but he wasn't feeling very well. He's in the back room."

He wanted to ask her if she had told him about Marilyn and Marcia. It would be better if he didn't, though, while the Barings were here. She was looking tired again, anyway. She had been lively when they were first talking. That was wearing off.

Skippy Baring wanted to know if he could talk to David for a while. He showed Skippy where the back room was, and where to turn on the light. He heard Mr. Baring trying to rouse his father. It didn't work, though. He heard his father's voice, but only for a second or two, and it was not clear. Mr. Baring stayed in his father's room for a time, without talking. And came on then back into the living room.

Mrs. Baring said they had to be leaving. Skippy and Mrs. Baring both said again that if there was anything they could do, to let them know. When they were leaving, he motioned his head for Lee to come along for a minute.

On the porch, he put something in Lee's shirt pocket. It was money, but he didn't look to see how much. "Thanks, Mr. Baring. Thanks a lot."

"That's okay, Colonel. You take it easy, you hear?"

"Yessir. Thanks a lot."

"You're sure now about this service station job? You said Brent's?"

"Yessir. He told me absolutely to be there."

"That's good. I'll see you, then."

He stood on the porch until they were driving away.

Strange. People like Skippy Baring. The ones like Fisher. Skippy still in his work clothes, needing a shave. Fisher in a suit and button-down shirt. A tie tack on his necktie. The trouble was, the ones like Skippy were outnumbered.

The ones like his father were.

What if it would have been better to go ahead and go with Marilyn and Marcia?

His mother was in the kitchen when he went back inside. She was sitting down.

"There's a little coffee left in the jar, Lee. I'd like to have some, if you would. I was going to make some, and then I thought I'd rest here for a minute."

Last week she had not wanted coffee, or anything else, unless he suggested it first. Sometimes not then.

He put water in the pot, and lit the gas burner under it.

Maybe it hadn't got through to her that Marilyn and Marcia were gone. She had not said anything about them. And if it hadn't, then it was better he had stayed here.

It was five dollars Skippy had given him. A five-dollar bill.

He put it back in his pocket. This was Thursday. Practically Friday. They could make it last till Monday, easy. And if he needed to, he could get George Brent to make an advance on his pay.

He could if he didn't get captured first. Mrs. B might still send somebody around.

Let her. He had got away once, he would again.

"What are you smiling at, Lee?"

"Oh—just the whole works, I guess."

He made the coffee, a cup for her and one for himself, and sat down with her. They could have another cup, and there would still be enough for breakfast.